VOW TO LOVE

A SWEET MARRIAGE OF CONVENIENCE ROMANCE

SHANAE JOHNSON

THOSE JOHNSON GIRLS

1

There was nothing like country air. Charlie Matthews took a deep inhale, filling his lungs with an abundance of the oxygen offered to him in this wide-open space. The sweet tang of honeysuckle tickled his nostrils. The musk of hay and horses clung to his upper lip. He gulped down more of the intangible substance until the smells left his lungs and permeated his heart.

Charlie was so used to breathing the processed air inside a cockpit. Up in the clouds, the sparse oxygen was clean, pure. It didn't smell like it belonged to anybody. Down here on earth, on the Flying Cross Ranch, it smelled like home. Because this was home.

He was home.

Charlie inhaled again, opening his mouth to take in even more of the scents of the ranch he'd spent much of his life on. The tang of manure touched his tongue. The perfume of wildflowers was a cloud around his nose. And best of all, the savory scents of a dozen casseroles stuffed into the fridge made his belly grumble.

By his inability to shut the fridge door without force, Charlie could easily estimate that everyone in Honor Valley had brought over a dish. All of his father's neighbors wanted to make sure that Haran Matthews had everything that he needed. Which was a change.

Not the notion of folks being neighborly. This was still a small town, after all. It was a change because, once upon a time, the community had been leery of the Matthews boys.

Just a decade ago, anytime a car would kick up gravel on its way down the drive of the Flying Cross Ranch, Charlie and his brothers would run into the woods and hide. Even if whatever damage had been done to whatever discarded piece of property, or ruffian's jaw, or pretty girl's misguided heart, wasn't their fault. Because if it was any one of their faults, then it was all of their faults. Their parents believed in group punishment as a deterrence.

It never worked. The singular thing that actually deterred the six sons of Haran and Tessa Matthews from their wicked ways and childish games was the day their beloved mother took ill and passed away far too suddenly for the boys to catch their breaths and process their loss.

"That's enough now, son," said Haran Matthews.

Charlie's father was propped up on the living room couch that overlooked the hundreds of acres of the family's land. The pillows Father Matthews's wife had sewn surrounded him, like plush soldiers flanking his every side. Charlie had been in the process of adding one more pillow to his father's back when the old man shooed away his intentions.

"I'm fine here," said Father Matthews. "Why don't you go out and see some of your old friends."

In this town, the only friends the Matthews boys had had been themselves. Well, that and the Silver sisters on the ranch next door, who were also social pariahs in this town. Charlie knew his father wasn't referring to his other sons or their next-door neighbors.

By old friends, Charlie knew exactly which friend his father meant. Seeing her was on his agenda soon. But not today.

Charlie reached out and covered his father with

a blanket that his mother had knit. The light blue fabric was in stark contrast against his father's brown skin. Charlie's pale hand was in contrast as well as he tucked the edges.

Father Matthews's hands were what Charlie loved best about his father. Those large, callused hands were what Charlie had noticed when he became Father Matthews's son twenty years ago. The man who would become his father had reached his hand out to Charlie, open-handed like they did on television shows where men dressed in suits and clasped hands.

The eight-year-old boy that Charlie had been had hesitated. He'd never shaken another person's hand before. He wasn't sure how to do it. Even before that, he wasn't used to any adult being kind to him. Somehow, he'd willed up enough courage to do that new and unknown thing. Taking Father Matthews's hand had been the best decision in his life.

"Don't the two of you have some pact where you have to be the first person each other sees when you're both back in town at the same time?"

The two of them did have that pact. This was the first time that Charlie would be breaking that promise to her. When she learned why, he knew she would forgive him.

She probably would forgive him.

She maybe would forgive him.

Hopefully, she would forgive him.

They'd made that pact when they were kids. They were adults now. Like him, she had grown used to adults breaking their promises over the years. This would be the one and only time he would break his promise to her.

His father had had a heart attack only a few days ago. Charlie had to take care of family first. Even though she had been his family before the Matthews had come in to rescue him from foster care.

That day had been the first time that Charlie had left her behind. It hadn't been the first time that she'd left him. Nor would it be the last.

For two decades, they'd been ships passing in the night. Docking a few days here and there. Rarely in the same port for too long. Today, Charlie was casting his anchor.

Which was entirely the wrong metaphor since, as an Air Force Pilot, he had hung up his wings before coming home. He was setting down his anchor, parking his boat, and mixing all the metaphors. The point was, Charlie Matthews was home to stay.

He took in another deep breath. This time breathing in the scent of his father.

Fresh pine.

Sweaty tack.

Safety.

Love.

"Just go and see her," said his father. "I'm just going to rest here."

For a man of the cloth, his father was actually a decent liar. Father Matthews uttered the bold-faced untruth with the peaceful air he'd use in a sermon. The problem was that Charlie had already caught him outside in the stables the other night. His father might not want to be babysat, but it's exactly what he needed.

"Nice try, old man. But I'm taking you in for your checkup today," said Charlie. "I have the rest of my life to spend with Savy."

Charlie thumbed the plastic ring he wore on a chain around his neck. He'd be seeing Savy soon. He'd be seeing her every day for the rest of his life after he got his father back on his feet.

2

____

It was times like these that Savy James felt like Cinderella. Here in this old, cluttered house, she scrubbed the floors and tended to the pots of food cooking on the stove. There weren't rats scuttling about in the walls, but a few ants had made their way inside since technically she lived in the wild. Unfortunately, unlike her girl Cindy, none of the wild creatures taking up space in and around Savy's home raised their voices in song or picked up a broom to help her clean.

Savy supposed that was fair. Her voice wasn't the delicate soprano of the Disney princess. She was an alto. Her voice was rich and full with a hint of smoke, though she'd never had a single cigarette. Still, she supposed with a voice slightly deeper than

Ursula in *The Little Mermaid*, the mice and wood-land creatures might think her a villain rather than the heroine.

They weren't the only ones.

"Yo, give it back. It's mine. 'Fore I drop you like a dime."

"You are so lame. You'll never make it as a rapper, not even for a candy bar."

"We gone see who be lame, when my records brings me fame."

"Ms. Savy's stupid rule says it's communal prop-erty, so it's not yours."

The shouted words were followed by a loud crash. The crash was the splintering of wood, not the break of bones. Savy had learned to distinguish those sounds at a young age. So, she didn't rush to the other room.

They were expecting an important guest soon, and the house was still in disarray. But she supposed it would look bad if she was mopping up blood when their visitor arrived. So, Savy decided to pick her battles. She rested the broom against the kitchen counter and walked calmly into the other room.

"Ashton, Denny," she said, raising her alto voice.

The commotion immediately stopped. It was

always jarring to others when Savy used the bass in her voice. She was technically a contra-alto, the lowest register for a female singer along the lines of Cher, Tina Turner, and Billie Holiday. However, if someone made her mad enough, she could reach the heavy tenor of Luciano Pavarotti. Most of the time, she had the smokey voice of the actress Kathleen Turner.

"If one of you kills the other, not only will that person have to clean up the blood, but I'll make you dispose of the body all by yourself. Do you hear me?"

The loud ruckus stopped abruptly, followed by two sulky, "Yes, Ms. Savy."

Had this been a Disney movie, she and the kids would've broken into a song and dance about cooperation and sharing. Savy could've pulled off the song. Not the dance. It wouldn't have mattered anyway because the two young boys scurried off in opposite directions.

The kids at the Bright Horizons foster home all hated chores. Which was entirely normal. All kids hated chores, especially if they involved a rag and a broom.

Not Savy.

Chores had been one of the few consistencies

in her life. As a young girl surrounded by the chaos of narcissistic and addicted parents, she'd clung to any routine and sense of normalcy. So, although Savy gave each of her charges daily chores at the foster home, she still went behind their work with a rag and a broom each night. It was the only way her mind settled enough for her to go to sleep.

Savy headed back to the kitchen to retrieve her broom as well as her zen, when another crash from a different room shook the walls. Once again, Savy let go of her trusty broom and went in search to see which hellion in her charge was trying to let loose the Devil in this house.

"Daria, what are you doing?"

That sopranic voice belonged to Savy's youngest sister. Along with her high-pitched voice, Foxy could've physically passed for a Disney princess with her wide eyes, button nose, and heart-shaped mouth. She most resembled Princess Jasmine with her golden tanned skin and raven braid hanging over her shoulder. All she needed was a tiara to complete the look. A tiara and a washcloth with lots of soap.

Foxy was bent over, looking up into the fireplace. She was covered from head to toe in soot, like she was the little Cinder girl instead of a runaway princess off on a magic carpet ride.

"What's going on?" said Savy.

"Daria climbed up the chimney," said Foxy.

"Oh, no," Savy groaned. "Not another superhero stunt."

"Remember that kid Neil who was here last year," came a disembodied voice from the chimney.

"Daria, get down from there," said Savy.

"He stole money and hid it somewhere in the house," said Daria. "But no one ever found it. I saw him in here, and he looked suspicious."

"Neil always looked suspicious," said Foxy. "Because he was always doing something he shouldn't."

"Which is why they took him to juvie after he stole from the library and tried to sell the books at the school book fair," said Savy.

"He was not the smartest," sighed Foxy, wiping the soot from her cheek, only to replace it with more streaks.

"Exactly," called down Daria. "I thought he hid the money he earned in the chimney."

Savy wanted to argue that money gained from thievery wasn't earned, but she had to keep her priorities straight. Once again, she picked her battles. "Daria, get down from there. You'll hurt yourself."

There was a sharp intake of breath that echoed down the chimney. Then a puff of soot. No child emerged.

"But, Ms. Savy, if I find the money, then we can buy the foster home from the government, and they can't take us away. We can all stay together."

If Neil had stashed money in the chimney, it wouldn't be enough. Because this house wasn't for sale. The land was being taken over by the government in favor of the protected wildlife in the valley. The herd of mustangs had tugged on the heartstrings of the community more than the wildlife inside the foster home. And now, they were the ones who had to fend for themselves.

"Daria, I need you to get down here now," said Savy, putting bass in her voice. "The representative from the government will be here any minute, and you're supposed to be in a dress with a clean face."

"A dress?"

There was another plume of soot. Along with a scuffling sound. Daria was likely climbing higher, more likely over the threat of a dress than a clean face.

"You'll need to get that, sis," said Foxy, canting her head toward the front hall.

Savy didn't ask for clarification. Foxy fancied herself a bit of a psychic. Their Creole grandmother had had the touch. Every once in a while, Foxy got a prediction right. When it came to expected visitors, her clairvoyant sister was batting a thousand.

As if on cue, the doorbell rang.

"I'll stall," said Savy. "You get her out of there. And then clean both of your faces."

Savy headed to the front door, but Ashton was already there. The kid wore a faded T-shirt with the explicit lyrics of a rap song that were blacked out. But the gist of the song was still easy to get by filling in the blanks. Savy believed in allowing the kids to express their personalities. She just wished she'd censored Ashton before he'd gotten to the door.

"What you at my door for? When you don't know the score?"

The brown-skinned man in a dollar store suit stepped back. He looked at the address, which was crazy, as this was the only house on the road. Then he looked again at the pint-sized wanna-be rapper with blond cornrows.

Savy had talked with Ashton—who insisted on

being called Ashtray—about manners, opening the door to strangers, and misappropriating other people's cultures. What Ashtray spat back was the notion that he had freedom of speech. And yes, he spat it all in rhyme. The kid walked around with a thesaurus and rhyming dictionary. Which was a boon to his education. So, Savy decided not to pick that battle.

The government official took one look at Ashtray, then Savy, then the mess left in the hall, and began to jot down some notes. This was not going well. She knew that if she didn't win this battle, then she might lose the entire war.

"Mr. Davidson, hi. I'm Savy James."

Savy gave the man her most winning smile. His facial features didn't crack as he regarded her. Before he could take her hand, a scream came from the other room. Then a thud. Followed by a plume of soot.

"I think I broke my arm," sobbed Daria.

Savy looked outside at the deserted road. A white horse ran in the distance, wild and free. There was no rider on its back. Even as she thumbed at the plastic ring she wore around her neck, she knew better than to wish for a prince to ride in and save her.

She knew Prince Charming existed. She'd found

her prince when she was a little girl. The problem was he never showed up at the right time, and he always left too soon. Forever was off in the future for her and Charlie Matthews. Forever definitely wasn't today when she needed him most.

3

"I can drive my own car, son."

"So I've heard. I hear you can fly a plane, too. But even the best pilots still need to be cleared for duty before they get back in the cockpit or behind a wheel."

Father Matthews didn't argue with his son. The man never argued. Just like always, he sat back and allowed his sons to experience the boons or consequences of their decisions.

When Charlie had wanted to speed on a country road, after Father Matthews said it was against the rules, the old man sat back and didn't say a word when the State Trooper pulled them over and gave Charlie a $150 speeding ticket. Neither did he give his son a penny toward the fine.

When Charlie decided he wanted to follow in his father's footsteps and go into the Air Force, his father sat back and smiled peacefully. He said nothing about the practical jokes that often cost Charlie clean underwear or the callout challenges that left him with a bloody nose that were hazing rituals of Basic Training.

To this day, Charlie obeyed speed limits on the road. Though he had broken the sound barrier in the air. He'd also earned the Flying Cross medal along with the respect of his fellow airmen. He took the lessons and the licks, just as his father taught him.

That was Haran Matthews's way. And Charlie loved the man for it. Father Matthews had somehow known that his boys wouldn't take to a hovering parent. But not one of them balked at having him as their copilot.

Charlie was in the driver's seat now as he pulled into the hospital parking lot. When he climbed out of the truck, his father followed suit. Father Matthews walked a bit slower, his shoulders a little slumped, but he managed to get into the hospital on his own power. All the while, Charlie hovered over him.

"Charlie Matthews, you're back."

Charlie looked up as one of the nurses broke from the reception desk and circumvented the line formed there to come over to him. She was blonde with porcelain skin that looked like it would burn if she got too close to the windows.

"It's me; Tina Billings. I was two years behind you at Honor Valley High."

"Right. Tina. Hey, long time." Charlie flashed a quick smile at the woman who he had no clue of ever meeting before. Certainly not ten years ago when he was consumed with thoughts of and stolen moments with Savy. "We're here for my father's appointment."

"Look at you, all grown up."

That threw Charlie off guard. Didn't she just say she was younger than he was? "Thanks, Tia. You, too. About my dad—"

"It's Tina." She wrapped her fingers around his biceps and squeezed. "You filled out in all the right places, didn't you?"

Charlie glanced over at his father. Of course, Haran Matthews said nothing. He simply stood to the side, barely hiding a grin at his son's discomfort.

"Is this your father?" Tina raised her voice and enunciated as she turned to Father Matthews. "Hello, Mr. Matthews. How are you today?"

Turnabout was fair play. Charlie grinned widely, saying nothing as Nurse Nia treated his dad like he was an invalid. For his part, Father Matthews looked over the woman's shoulder, like he was playing the senile role she'd cast for him.

"You're such a good son, Charlie." The nurse fixed her sights back on the younger Matthews. "You're going to make a good father."

"Yeah, probably because I was raised by a good man. The one standing here who just had a heart attack a couple of days ago. You think we can get him a wheelchair?"

"I don't need a wheelchair, son. I see Dr. Nelson down the hall. I can get to his office all by myself. Why don't you stay here and talk with your old friend."

Grin restored, Father Matthews whistled as he made his way down the hallway. Charlie would've cursed the man if he didn't know for sure that God was on Father Matthews's side. Watching his father, Charlie couldn't help but wonder if his steps weren't as sure as they'd always been? Did his shoulders droop a bit? Was that a hunch in his back?

The guilt that Charlie had been harboring since learning of his father's condition while he was hundreds of miles away washed over him again.

He'd been gone for such a long time this time. But it couldn't be helped. There had been orders. If his father had taught him anything, it was that a soldier should excel at his orders.

So Charlie had. And with each mission accomplished, he'd been given another. And then another.

Now his flying days were over. This was his new mission. His final mission. To get his family's house in order. That would start with his father, and it would end with the woman he loved.

"So, what do you think?"

Charlie blinked. He looked down to see that Nurse Telia had a hand on his chest and another snaking around his neck. He'd missed the entire thread of the one-sided conversation she'd been having with him. Likely because he'd forgotten she was even there. Because there was only one woman Charlie Matthews had ever been interested in for his whole life.

And there she was.

Like he'd called her to him, Savy James came in through the sliding glass doors of the hospital. Like every single time Charlie had seen the woman, beginning all the way back when she'd been an eight-year-old girl with ashy knees, dirt under her fingernails, and a mean purse to her lips, she took his breath away.

Her tan skin that reminded him of spun gold. Her raven curls that no comb could ever tame. Those long legs that outpaced him when they were young had mesmerized him as he grew up. Even with her long legs, she wasn't a tall woman. Savy came up to Charlie's chest, right where his heart beat. It kicked into high gear at the sight of the first person to ever make it race.

He'd planned to go to Bright Horizon's in the morning. Probably later tonight, after he'd made sure his father was snug in bed. Now he wouldn't have to wait. She was here. In front of him. Within his reach.

Charlie took a step toward her. He didn't get far. Something was holding him back. Something was holding onto him.

Charlie couldn't tear his gaze away from Savy to find out what. Those charcoal-gray eyes landed on him. Even from across the room, he felt the electricity zap between them. Above, the fluorescent light flickered. Outside, the sun broke through clouds.

Savy held him still with her gaze. Or maybe the

world held still around him. Charlie didn't know. He didn't care.

What he did care about was the frown on Savy's face. Why was her gaze narrowing? Why were her lips pursing?

Charlie knew every look and quirk of this woman's face. She was upset with him. But he hadn't done anything. He hadn't even said a word. It was far too soon in their reunion for her to be angry with him.

There was usually the breathless moment when they came back into each other's presence. Followed by a moment of awkwardness. Then there was kissing.

Oh, he wanted to skip straight to the kissing. It was his favorite thing to do in the world. Flying was a distant second to the weightless joy he found against Savy's lips.

Charlie wanted to take flight. But something was holding him down. Finally, he looked over and remembered the excess baggage hanging off his bicep.

4

There was a saying in the South. It was a saying about how women clutched their pearls when they were shocked. Savy wasn't a fan of pearls. They were the guts of an oyster. She'd never taken to the idea of wearing an animal's innards on her body.

Still, when she saw Charlie Matthews embracing Tina Billings, her hand immediately went to her throat. There weren't any pearls there. Just the thin gold chain with a piece of plastic dangling from the end.

It was the plastic that was priceless. A prize won from a Cracker Jack box years ago. A promise given to her with sugary fingers and a sweet smile.

Savy clung to that pact as she watched the impossible play out right before her eyes.

Charlie Matthews was home. He was back in Honor Valley.

That wasn't the impossible part. He always came back. He just never stayed. Not since he'd enlisted in the Air Force. He was always being called away on a mission.

Which she supposed she should be pleased about. It meant he was good at his job. It meant he was indispensable to their country. He was indispensable to her, too, and he'd enlisted his services to her first. Surprisingly, the U.S. Government did not respect the dibs of an eight-year-old girl.

But he was home right now. Which baffled Savy because she hadn't been the first person to know about his return. She was always the first to know. It was part of their pact.

The pact that started after the first time her mother, who had abandoned them months before that, snatched Savy, Foxy, and Tricksy out of the foster home to go on the road with her as backup singers. When her mom overdosed after a show in Vegas, the girls had been taken and returned to the foster care home. Charlie had snuck into their room and held her hand tight until the morning when he'd been found and confined to his room during free time. They'd lost those three days apart, but they were back together again. Until her mom got clean and came back to reclaim them for a show in L.A.

From that point on, it was a series of hits and misses with the two of them. Her mom would go on a bender, and Savy would return to Honor Valley, only to find that Charlie was away at summer camp. Or Charlie would be home on leave, only to come home and find that she was back on the road singing with her sisters.

The stars had trouble aligning for Savy James and Charlie Matthews. Looking at him now, as he stood under the fluorescent lights of the hospital, the impossible glared back at Savy. Charlie Matthews—her Charlie Matthews—was embracing another woman. A woman who wasn't her.

"Back again, Savy?"

Savy broke her gaze from the impossible scene on display down the hall and focused on the intake nurse. The gray-haired woman reminded Savy of her second-grade teacher. All the kids swore Mrs. September was actually the witch in Hansel and Gretel. Nurse Ruddell had the same grimace on her wrinkled face when she glared down at Daria.

"What was it this time, Daria? Trying to fly? Trying to walk through walls? Or proving you're impervious to pain by putting your hand in a fire?"

Mr. Davidson raised both eyebrows to his hairline. The fingers of his right hand twitched as though he wanted to jot down some more incriminating notes about Savy's foster kids. Luckily, he couldn't reach for his pen and notepad. His hands had a Daria-sized bundle in them.

Daria held her upper lip stiffly. Her red cape hung limp at her back, covered in soot. She was always surprised when she bled, bruised, or broke a bone like a normal human.

"This has happened before?" asked Mr. Davidson.

"That child's in here every other week," supplied Nurse Ruddell. "She thinks she's a superhero. She's got a medical record like a rap sheet. If I hadn't seen her antics firsthand, I would've called CPS."

Nurse Ruddell chucked her head to the side to indicate Savy. Little did Nurse Ruddell know, Mr. Davidson was worse than Child Protective Services. A few more unfavorable notes written down about Savy and her kids, and these children would be let loose in the wild. Wrangling the wild horses running in the valley would be simpler than trying to tame them.

"I encourage my charges to develop a healthy imagination," Savy said.

"One that requires stitches and casts," Nurse Ruddell said as she placed the hospital intake band around Daria's arm. She hadn't even bothered to hand Savy any intake forms. They were in here so much that the nurses knew the kid's details by heart.

"I'm okay, Ms. Savy," Daria said as Mr. Davidson deposited her into the wheelchair offered by Nurse Ruddell. "I'm sorry I didn't find the money in the chimney."

"You told this child to go looking for money in a chimney?" Mr. Davidson turned to Savy in horror.

"No, I di—"

He was already scribbling more notes down on his pad now that his hands were free. Nurse Ruddell was wheeling Daria down the hall for an x-ray. Savy stood in the middle of the reception area, flustered and defeated.

She couldn't lose these kids. She was all they had. No one else wanted them. Savy knew because she'd tried to place each of them in a permanent home. One by one, they came back to her, returned to sender. Two families quit fostering after taking in Denny and Daria.

Savy had promised the kids would always have a home at Bright Horizons. It had been the one place that was constant in her life. Which was why when she retired from singing at the ripe old age of twenty-two, she'd taken over Bright Horizons. And now it, along with the children, was in danger of being taken from her.

She hadn't felt this alone since the first time she returned to Honor Valley, and Charlie was overseas, entirely beyond her reach.

Then warm arms were around her. Followed by a warm, familiar smell. Those strong arms fit her snug and tight. That smell brought about instant peace and calm. Then came the voice she heard every night in her dreams.

"Hey."

It was just one word. Just one syllable. It meant nothing. It meant everything.

Savy had been holding herself so tightly wound these last few days. She couldn't break. Everyone needed her to be strong.

Not him.

He was the strong one. In his arms was the only place she could show her weaknesses. He was the soft place that absorbed her harsh edges. His was the gentle voice that softened her tenor.

Savy slumped into Charlie's body. Her feet left the ground as she allowed him to whisk her away like her very own Prince Charming. When she opened her eyes, they were alone in an exam room.

A gurney with ripped paper covering the hard cushion. A heart monitor that showed a flat line. A tissue on the floor that had missed the waste disposal bin.

And Charlie.

Her Charlie.

Here. With her. As it should be.

Savy pulled his head down to hers, and she was kissing him. He was kissing her. They were kissing one another.

The only time her world made sense was in this man's arms. When she was gazing into his eyes. When he was whispering in her ear how much he adored her. Those few moments in her lifetime that the stars aligned and everything else fell away.

The overhead fluorescent light made a buzzing noise, interrupting the soundtrack of soft sighs that accompanied this reunion. The light blinked out and in, like a fading star. When it flicked back on, shining its full force, Savy broke the kiss.

"You're dating Tina Billings?"

"Who?"

"The woman who had her hands all over you."

"What woman?"

Charlie asked the question, likely more out of the politeness hammered into him by his adoptive parents. He clearly wasn't interested in the answer. Because he was kissing Savy again.

That kiss told Savy loud and clear everything she needed to know about what she thought she'd seen. There had been nothing between Charlie and Tina. Savy knew there had never been anything between Charlie and any other woman that wasn't her.

She didn't doubt his fidelity. He didn't doubt hers. The first time they'd laid eyes on each other, both their hearts had shouted *this one.*

They'd both been eight when they met. They'd been thirteen when they'd shared their first kiss. They'd been sixteen the first time Charlie proposed to her.

Saying yes to Charlie Matthews wasn't the problem. Being with him was.

"You're here," Savy said, placing her hand on his chest. She felt the same thin chain and the same plastic ring that she wore around her neck.

"I am." Charlie grinned that devastating grin that kept her heart locked down from every man who came near.

"How long?" She hated to ask it, but she had to know. She had to get her expectations set. She had to know how long she could rest in heaven before she was flung back down to earth when he left. "How long?" she repeated.

"Forever."

There had been soft sighs coming from her mouth only a second ago. With that single word, a gush of hot air burst from her chest and out of her mouth. Her nostrils flared but not with desire. Savy pressed her hands against Charlie's chest, ignoring his racing heart, and shoved him away from her. Hard.

5

Charlie didn't budge when Savy pushed him away. Oh, his girl was strong. He'd made sure of that. Racing with her through the woods when they were kids. Challenging her to push up and pull up contests when they were teens. And teaching her self-defense moves when they were new adults.

There was no way he was leaving her unprotected in this world. Not with what they'd seen growing up in the system. Especially not with her addict of a mother dragging the girls off to seedy concert halls and dives.

If he hadn't been sure that Savy could hold her own, Charlie doubted he would've been able to be away from her for such long stretches. He also knew this weak display of her power had to do more with emotion than an actual desire to send him away.

So he held on. He had too many years of practice holding on to this woman to let such a flimsy shove push him away. Now that he was here to stay, he was not letting her go.

"This is because I broke our pact?" He squeezed her tighter. "Because I didn't come to you first."

"I didn't expect you to come to me first, you big oaf." She stopped her ineffectual shoving and splayed her hand over his heart. "Your dad had a heart attack. Of course, you would go straight to him."

"Right." Charlie pressed a kiss to her temple, breathing in the scent of her. Cinnamon and bleach and Savy. "So, what are you mad about?"

"You said forever."

Her voice was a whisper. A shaky whisper. A shaky whisper that rattled through him and tucked in behind his chest.

"It's never forever with the two of us," she continued on in that whisper, as though she was afraid of being overheard. "It's always for a short time. And that's fine."

Her voice trembled on the word fine. It sounded as though her teeth chattered as they pressed against her bottom lip to make the F sound. The rest of the word came out as though it was made of smoke.

It was not fine.

It was forever.

Charlie had said forever. He'd said forever to her since he'd looked the word up in a dictionary and decided it applied to the two of them. And now, he could finally live up to that definition.

"It's true," said Charlie. "I'm out."

"Out?"

"Out of the Air Force and back home. For good."

"What do you mean *for good*?"

He meant forever. But she'd already shoved at him with that word, so he couldn't repeat it. Instead, Charlie pressed more kisses to her temple as though he were anointing his queen with a crown of affection.

"It means exactly what it sounds like, Sav. I hung up my wings."

Charlie pulled back from Savy, then he pulled the chain that hung beneath his shirt out. He traced the links until he came to the ring attached. There were two rings on there. The first one was the plastic ring that mirrored hers. The second had a real diamond.

"I wanted to do this in front of our families, but now's a good a time as ever."

"Charlie—" Savy choked. Her lips stayed parted, but no other words came out of her mouth. Even better, she kept her hands to herself.

Charlie sank down to one knee. This was his favorite view of her. Looking up at Savy as she loomed large over him. This woman had always loomed large over him.

She was his moonlight, his sunshine. If it had been ancient times, he would've been one of the idolators who worshipped the sun or moon goddess. He was entirely certain that God had put Savy on this earth as a brag about how perfect His craftsmanship truly was.

"Savy James, I have loved you since before I knew what the word meant."

Savy's hands reached down to cup Charlie's face. She tilted his head back so that she could peer directly into his eyes. He grinned at her machinations, having no trouble staring right back at the woman he loved and baring his soul to her.

Savy's charcoal-gray eyes glistened with unshed tears. She shook her head slowly from side to side. Charlie knew she wasn't denying him. She'd already said yes the first time he'd proposed when they were sixteen. This was just a formality.

"Would you do me the honor of—"

"No!" Savy snatched her hands away from his head and planted them on her hips. It was her matronly pose, the one she used when her sisters or any of the Matthews boys got out of line. She'd never used it on Charlie.

Charlie's head jerked to the side to get a different view of her. "Beg your pardon?"

"I said no."

"Sav, I'm asking you to marry me."

"I know."

Charlie stood then. He took in a deep inhale, letting the air settle past his chest and down into his gut. "You're saying no?"

"I am."

Why would she say no to him? They were destined to be married, to be together for the rest of their lives.

He reached for her again. She hesitated, but it was only perfunctory. She put up no resistance when he wrapped her in his embrace, their lips less than an inch apart.

"I don't get it?" said Charlie.

Savy pursed her lips in the universal language of

I'm about to explain it to you. She didn't get a chance to explain anything because the door to the exam room opened up.

"There you are, Ms. James."

A dark-skinned man in an ill-fitting suit poked his head in the door. He took one look at Savy and frowned. Then his glance turned to Charlie, which only served to deepen the frown.

"The child is asking for you," he sneered. "And I find you making out in a closet with a man."

"We weren't making out," said Savy.

"We were making out," said Charlie.

"He was just asking me to marry him again," Savy said dismissively. Then, once again, she shoved at Charlie's chest in a weak attempt to break free. "Charlie, not now."

Savy shoved again, this time with real force, as though she was actually trying to get away from him. What was going on?

"You're engaged to this man?" asked the suit.

"Yes," said Charlie.

"No," said Savy.

The man ignored Savy and eyed Charlie. "Well, that does change things a bit."

"Excuse me?" said Savy.

"Change what?" said Charlie.

The man jotted notes down on a pad as he spoke. "What those children need is a man's firm hand in the home."

Charlie wasn't exactly sure what was going on. But he was pretty good at math. Adding up the man's ill-fitting suit told Charlie that this was clearly a government employee. Plus the note-taking on a yellow legal pad? Definitely a bureaucrat. Altogether, this pointed to something happening at the foster home.

"That's me," said Charlie. "I have a firm hand. And I plan to be in the home."

This must be Savy's hesitation. He knew she'd do anything for the kids under her care. She'd been the same way when they were kids, taking each new foster kid under her wing. She'd tried to do that to Charlie when he'd arrived at Bright Horizons. But they both soon learned that his wingspan was broader than hers.

So, this official was doing a report on the foster home. Well, Charlie would be happy to move in there after he and Savy got married. It would allow him to be with the woman he loved, help the kids, and take care of his father.

It was perfect.

"I'll take your engagement under advisement and put it in my report."

The bureaucrat gave Charlie a nod. Charlie held out his hand to the man and shook. It was a weak handshake, which told Charlie everything else he needed to know about the man.

"I'll see you back at the foster home," said the weak-handed man with a sour glance at Savy. He turned on his heel and walked out the door.

When Charlie turned back to Savy, her glance at him was sour.

"What?" he asked. "This is perfect. We'll get married and live in the foster home. Meanwhile, I'll be within driving distance to help my dad on the ranch every day."

"The foster home is being demolished."

"What?"

"Bright Horizon's isn't going to be here in the valley anymore. They're moving it across the state."

6

"They're moving the foster home?" Charlie leaned back against the door. He crossed his arms over his broad chest.

Savy had spent cool afternoons in the sun basking in the comfort of that chest. He'd wrapped those strong biceps around her as they lay out on a blanket, staring at the clouds. The memory of Tina Billings hanging off Charlie's arm was a distant wisp of the past. That space at Charlie's heart, that nook between his neck and his shoulder, that spot at the underside of his chin, all those places belonged to Savy.

Right now, she desperately wanted back inside those arms. The day had been trying enough with

Daria and Mr. Davidson. And then this fool had to go and propose to her.

"Why are they moving Bright Horizons?" Charlie asked.

"Tilly."

It was a one-word answer. A name that anyone in Honor Valley would understand and need no more explanation for.

"Of course." Charlie pinched the bridge of his nose. It was a common move seen whenever anyone in the valley came up against that particular Silver sister. "Let me guess; one of Tilly's petitions to save the wildlife?"

Charlie let go of his nose. His hand didn't go back to his side. It went to hers. His fingertips grazed the waistband of her pants.

He didn't tug. He didn't need to. The two of them were magnets. They always found one another.

So, of course, Savy took a step toward him. "Tilly filed a petition to have the wild horses of the valley protected by the government. She did it back in high school. Ten years later, and it's reared up to bite us."

Charlie's arms were around her now. Savy's head found her way to the space at his heart. It beat loud and strong, just as it had when they were little kids.

Charlie Matthews had always had a big heart, and he always saved the most space for her.

"Now that the land is protected for the horses, they're moving the foster home," said Charlie. It wasn't a question. The words were said without inflection. As though they were just meant to fill the silence. Or perhaps to distract her.

She had somewhere to be. But for the life of her, she couldn't remember where. Savy shifted from the center of Charlie's heart to the nook between his neck and shoulder.

"I'm trying to stay with the kids, to keep them together." Savy's lips brushed the underside of Charlie's chin and held there. She'd missed the smell of him. Irish Spring soap, salt, and her Charlie.

"And The Suit's in charge of that decision?"

Savy giggled at that nickname. "He does wear an awful suit."

"Doesn't suit him."

She giggled again, raising her head to glance up at Charlie. She had forgotten how devastatingly handsome the man she loved was. Even with tons of pictures in albums and on her phone, not a single one of them did the man's actual beauty justice.

Dark hair that had grown just a little too long for military regulation. Dark eyes with that ring of hazel that always made her feel he was shining a light on her when he gazed at her. Those lips that always rested in a half-smile.

Those lips.

That smile.

Those lips.

Charlie smiled fully, stretching his lips until his white teeth flashed at her. "God, you're beautiful. I forget how beautiful you are in the flesh. When I see you in my mind, it's a pale comparison. Even the pictures I have of you don't do you any real justice."

That was all it took. Savy snaked her hand into his curls. She gripped hard as she tugged his head down. Charlie came willingly. His lips crashed down on hers.

The impact was powerful enough to destroy them. Instead, it set Savy soaring. Kissing Charlie Matthews had always made her feel weightless and carefree.

Except she couldn't be carefree. She couldn't fly away. Not now. There would be collateral damage left on the ground.

"The kids," she breathed when she broke the kiss.

"Everything is going to be fine, Sav."

Charlie took her hands in his. She felt something cold and metallic against her palm and then over her finger. Looking down, she saw the diamond ring. It felt heavy on her hand.

Savy had dreamed of Charlie proposing to her. He'd done it before. Those other times they'd been kids, not fully in charge of their living situations.

Now they were adults. He was out of the military. She was no longer on the road touring as a singer with her sisters. But she wasn't free to fly away with him.

The kids.

Savy had to go where these kids went. She was all they had. She couldn't let them break the siblings up. She and her sisters had fought so hard to stick together when they were that age. Who knew what would've happened to them if they got split up.

She knew Charlie understood that. The only reason his brothers had made it to adulthood in one piece and not behind bars was because they'd been able to stick together. That, and they had the Matthews as foster parents.

"I came home to marry you," said Charlie.

"You can't marry me."

"I am going to marry you."

"Charlie—"

"Isn't it a part of your job description to make

kids believe they can be anything when they grow up?"

"We're not kids anymore, Charlie."

"You're right. We're grown up. This is exactly what I wanted to be when I grew up. Now I'm all grown up. I came home to finally be with you."

"I'm leaving Honor Valley."

"Then I'm coming with you."

"Really?"

"Really."

"Truly?"

"Yes, Sav."

"How's your dad?"

That stopped him short. Father Matthews needed his son's help. Savy had seen the man just days before the heart attack, and he hadn't looked as spry then. Haran Matthews was getting on in his years. He couldn't move around the ranch the way he had a decade ago.

He needed his family. He needed his sons. He needed Charlie.

Once again, forever took another step into the future for her and Charlie. It wasn't going to happen today.

"Sav," Charlie reached for her.

Savy moved out of his reach, out of the one place

in the world that always made her feel safe, even if only for the short bursts of time they had together.

"It's not our time," she said.

How many times had they said that to each other over the years? When would it be time for them to be in the same place at the same time? Would it ever happen?

"Sav."

"Your dad needs you, and those kids need me."

"I need you."

Savy shook her head. "I have to go."

Charlie pulled her back to him. She let him, too tired to fight it. She rested another second at the space at his heart and listened to his heartbeat. She turned her head into the nook between his neck and shoulder and inhaled the scent of him. She lifted her lips to the spot at the underside of his chin and gave him a kiss farewell.

"I love you forever," she whispered.

"I love you always."

He didn't fight her when she backed away. This part was as familiar as the kissing. It was familiar as his scent. They always had to say goodbye sooner or later.

7

———

harlie watched Savy walk away. He was tired of that sight. He wanted the sight of her coming into his arms. Of her looking comfortable and secure because he'd taken her worries away. Savy's shoulders slumped as she moved down the hall.

This was all wrong. Today was supposed to be the start of their forever. Instead, it felt like they were even further apart than yesterday.

Charlie knew he needed to give Savy space. She didn't do well when pressured. He also knew there was no way he was letting the woman of his dreams get away from him.

Against his better judgment, he took a step toward her. However, instead of flying off toward his only destination, he felt a heavy weight tethering him in place.

"Charlie Matthews, you naughty boy. You disappeared on me."

Charlie turned to see Nurse Tia hanging off his bicep. The situation looked vaguely familiar. Then he realized that this was the woman Savy had been referring to earlier.

Was the nurse coming onto him? Charlie wasn't sure. He'd never been able to read the cues correctly because he'd never paid attention to any woman who wasn't Savy.

When he looked back in the direction Savy had walked off, she was gone. Fine. He'd let her slip away today. He'd be back in fighting form tomorrow.

"Where's my father?"

"He's nearly done with his checkup." Nurse Nina snaked her hands from his bicep to his chest. "I was coming to find you."

Charlie stepped out of her embrace and around her. She was a petite little thing, but she had arms everywhere. "Just point me to his room."

"This is his prescription." She held up a small square of a paper with a doctor's illegible chicken scratch on it. "And this is my number." She held up a pink Post-it note with unmistakable clear block letters and numbers.

"What for?"

"Wow, you have been gone for a long time." She sidled back up to him, cornering Charlie against the door where he and Savy had shared their all-too-brief reunion. "When a girl gives you her phone number, she wants you to call her to take her out on a date."

"I don't date."

"It's easy. I'll show you how."

"I've never been interested in learning how."

Finally, it looked like he was getting somewhere with her. Nurse Telia leaned away from him, her features crinkled. "Are you... gay?"

"Engaged. Since I was about sixteen." And he would be getting married soon. He'd managed to slip a diamond ring on Savy's finger, so he'd say that was progress.

"Ha, that's funny," singsonged the nurse.

Hadn't she said they went to school together? If they had, then she would know that Charlie Matthews had been completely, totally, and solely head over heels in love with Savy James since, well, forever.

"Where did you say my father was?"

"Right here, son."

Another nurse wheeled his father down the corridor in a wheelchair. This nurse was doing her job, fussing over Father Matthews instead of flirting with his son. The man who had been the hero of Charlie's life looked older, frailer sitting in the rolling chair.

When Charlie had left home for the service, Father Matthews had still been strong. He'd had his other sons to help him on the ranch. For the last five years, his father had been all alone with all that land. In the state he was in now, he definitely couldn't manage the ranch alone.

Charlie looked back toward the hall where Savy had disappeared. The urge to follow her was still strong. It always would be. But he couldn't leave his father behind. Not now.

Savy and Charlie's forever would just have to wait a little while longer to begin.

Father Matthews was looking down at his pocket watch. Charlie didn't need to come closer to know what picture was inside of the watch. It was his wife.

Haran and Tessa Matthews had had a love so bright that Charlie and his brothers had had to hide their eyes the first few months they lived at Flying Cross. It had been gross the way the two carried on, stealing kisses, always smiling when the other came in the room, saying crazy things like *I Love You.*

Charlie got over the grossness of it before his other brothers did. Because Charlie recognized that the way his foster father looked at his foster mother was the way he felt when he looked at Savy.

Charlie came over and put an arm around his father as he rose from the wheelchair. Thankfully, the older man didn't protest.

"What took you so long?" Father Matthews asked.

"I was talking to Savy."

"Savy's here?" His father perked up. "Oh wait, don't tell me? Is it the little superhero again?"

"Superhero?"

Father Matthews's eyes crinkled the way they did when one of his sons made him laugh. "One of her kids thinks she's a superhero. She's in and out of the emergency room every month. Worse than your brother, Joe."

Joe had loved comics growing up. He'd gone into the military to be a hero. He'd never seen a day of combat in his role once there. Now he was setting his sights on politics. He didn't like it when Charlie pointed out that many of the villains in the comics were politicians.

"How'd things go with you and Savy?" Father asked as they stepped out of the hospital's sliding glass door.

"Same as usual."

"That bad?"

Father Matthews clapped Charlie on the back. Charlie jerked forward. His father's heart might've faltered a few days ago, but he still had the same strength in his hands.

"She said they're moving the foster home across the state."

"Oh." Father Matthews's hand splayed on Charlie's back. Just as his father's strength was still there, so was the instant comfort that spread from his fingers and into Charlie's chest.

"She's trying to make sure she and her sisters stay on at the home."

Father Matthews nodded as the two men crossed into the street, walking side by side. "Savy's been with those kids for the last five years. Foxy joined her just last year. I think Tricksy is still out on the road singing, but she makes it back to the valley from time to time."

"Savy's the best man for the job."

His father nodded at that pronouncement.

When he and his brothers were kids, everyone

lined up behind Charlie. Charlie always lined up behind Savy. Because he followed her everywhere. He would follow her across the state if he had to. He just had to get his father back on his feet first. Of course, that's when the old man stumbled.

"Dad." Charlie flung out his hands, but his father had already righted himself.

They both looked down to see what had caused the stumble. It was a skateboard. A sulking kid was walking toward them.

"Watch it," Charlie shouted. "You could hurt somebody."

The kid narrowed his eyes at Charlie, his body tense as though ready to put up a fight. The little pipsqueak couldn't have been more than five feet and a hundred pounds to Charlie's over six feet and two-hundred pounds. But when the kid's eyes reached his father, the rascal's look softened.

"Sorry, Father Matthews."

"What are you doing out here, Denny?"

Denny stepped on the edge of the skateboard. The board flipped up and landed in his open palm. "I was looking for my sister."

"I don't see the foster van," said Father Matthews as he looked around.

Charlie gave the kid a second glance. He did

have all the hallmarks of a foster kid. Scuffed shoes, frayed edges at the neck of his shirt, and shifty eyes that said he didn't trust any adult.

Denny glared at Charlie. Charlie glared right back. From his years in the system, he knew he had to establish dominance quickly, and size and age didn't matter.

"I think you may have missed Ms. Savy and your sister," said Father Matthews when his gaze returned to the kid. "We'll give you a ride home, won't we, son?"

That question had an easy answer. Charlie would use any reason to see Savy. Even if it meant dragging this little thug along for the ride.

8

$\mathscr{B}$y the time Savy put the van in park back at Bright Horizons, the sun was starting to set. It had been a long day. A long week. A long lifetime. And she was tired.

Charlie Matthews was home. For good. And because their timing was epically awful, she was the one leaving this time.

The only thing she wanted to do was curl up inside a set of strong arms, lay her head against a strong chest with a heart that beat just for her, and steal kisses at the underside of a chin with a five o'clock shadow. Too bad she just walked away from the only man who met all those descriptors.

For the first part of their lives, it had always been her leaving. Not that she'd had any choice. Her mother would inevitably get herself clean, get a gig featuring her and her daughters as backup singers, and scoop them out of foster care. After a month or two—the longest stretch being a full year—Fanny James would just as inevitably relapse, lose the gig, and get her kids taken from her again.

The cycle continued until Savy's eighteenth birthday. Ten years of instability. No child should've survived that. But she and her sisters did.

Many of the kids she now fostered had had similar beginnings in their lives. Ashton was born an addict. His mom was still out on the street making money on her back. LaTisha had spent the first six months of her life in the Neonatal unit because of the drugs in her mother's system. Denny and Daria had never actually slept on a bed until they came to the foster home. Miguel had been from a loving family, but his family had wanted more for him, and so they'd sent him to the border at the tender age of five in search of that better life.

In some ways, her kids had had it worse than Savy had. But Savy was determined to give them the best that she could. She was going to lose the house; she accepted that. What she would not accept was having those five kids taken from her. They could find another house and make it their home, as long as they stuck together.

The door to the van flew open, and a small body whizzed out, a cape flying behind her.

"Daria, slow down!"

"Yes, Ms. Savy," called the kid, whose pace slowed only a fraction.

Daria still moved as fast as a little rabbit, even with the ankle brace. Her foot wasn't broken, only a sprain. It would likely be broken by the morning if the child kept up that pace.

"We have a problem, sis."

Four out of five of those were Savy's least favorite words. She decided to focus on her favorite word, sis.

Savy loved being a sister. Even more, she loved being a big sister. Managing Foxy and Tricksy from such a young age had cemented what Savy was going to do with her life. Though she had a voice that could bring down an auditorium, it was best used at wrangling underaged hellions.

Foxy had certainly been a hellion in her youth. She'd only calmed down over the last couple of years. She was an invaluable addition to the foster home staff and came to love the kids as much as Savy did.

"Denny's missing."

Why couldn't Foxy have said the pipes had burst? That would've been an easier situation to deal with on the day a government official came a' knocking. Or better yet, that the house was on fire. That would've been a far more manageable problem at the moment.

Where Daria wanted to fly, her older brother wanted to disappear. They had trouble with Denny sneaking off. But he always came back. This was the worst time for him to pull a stunt.

"You check all the usual places?" asked Savy, getting out of the van.

"I did. He's not outside on the land. I called around to a couple of stores, but Mr. Finke hung up on me, and Mrs. Rhule said she'd call the police if she saw him."

There was a tension headache brewing at Savy's temples. This was just what she needed. A hospital visit, followed by picking up a kid at the police station while her fitness as a foster mom was under scrutiny.

Foxy reached up and gave Savy's temples a rub, bless her soul. "I know, sis, it's the last thing we need right now when Mr. Clicky Pen is here. But it could be worse. He could've seen one of us making out with some random guy."

Savy whipped her head out of her sister's hold. Foxy wasn't looking at her. Had she been joking? Did she know that Charlie was back? That was the only man Savy had ever kissed.

Tricksy was the only James sister that had had more than one boyfriend. Was Tricksy back? Her middle sister returning at this point in time was only slightly better than a house fire.

"Ms. James," called Mr. Davidson as he jogged down the steps, click pen in hand. "I have nearly everything I need to start my report. I just need to interview the fifth child, Dennis."

"He won't answer to that," called Daria. "His name is Denny."

Mr. Davidson ignored the little girl and focused on Savy. "Where is the child?"

Savy swallowed. This was it. She was going to lose these kids. They'd been counting on her, and she was about to let them all down.

She opened her mouth, but before she could get a single word out, she choked. Dust from a truck kicking up rocks on the gravel drive pulled up to them. Savy immediately recognized the old beat-up truck. She'd spent many an evening on the flatbed of that truck making out with Charlie.

Charlie sat in the driver's seat now. His father in the passenger seat. And... was that Denny in the back?

Charlie climbed out first. Savy had the instinct to run to the man. To fling herself into his arms and bury her face in his chest. But this was not the time for that. Charlie had provided her with an out, and she grabbed for it.

"I'm sorry, Mr. Davidson," she said. "I forgot to tell you that Denny was out with my fiancé."

Foxy looked from Charlie and back to her sister. Savy sent her daggers to hold her tongue. It wasn't a lie. She and Charlie had always planned to get married. Some day. Though some day never turned out to be today.

For his part, Charlie came up and put an arm around her. Savy's body sagged into his chest. She couldn't help it. It was exactly what she needed. So was the kiss he placed at her temple.

Her tension headache disappeared with the press of his lips. Savy let out a low sigh. She couldn't help it. Whenever she was in Charlie's arms, all of her cares went away.

"I don't believe we were formally introduced,"

said Charlie. "Captain Charles Matthews. And this is my father, Captain Haran Matthews. I believe you were looking for Denny. Sorry, we were just having some man-to-man time."

"Why weren't we invited?" came Miguel's voice.

"Yo, that's unfair," rapped Ashton. "That time shoulda been shared."

There was that headache knocking at Savy's right temple. Charlie squeezed her tighter, resting his chin at the top of her head. The pain dissipated like a whisper.

Mr. Davidson clicked his pen and jotted down more notes. "Military men; that's what these kids need. A strong hand to guide them. It's good to know these kids will have a strong hand guiding them when we move you across the state."

Savy sank deeper into Charlie's chest. Just when she thought she might skate by, it was all about to be taken away from her again.

She could have Charlie if she left the kids. Or better yet, she could have Charlie and keep the kids if Charlie came with them. Neither of those situations was tenable. The reason why spoke up to confirm it.

"There's been a misunderstanding," said Father Matthews. "My son isn't moving across the state. He and his future wife will be moving their family onto our ranch."

"The ranch?" both Savy and Charlie said in unison. The surprise was loud in each of their voices.

For his part, Mr. Davidson clicked his pen so that the point retracted. It looked like he was done taking notes. Instead, Mr. Davidson nodded, as though Father Matthews's statement made it all a done deal.

9

———

The children eyed Charlie curiously. Well, the two girls did. The one with the cape—Daria, he'd learned her name was—and ankle brace cocked her head to the right and then to the left, eyes squinting like Christopher Reeve used to do in the Superman movies when he was using his laser vision. Charlie rubbed a hand just under his chin where it felt a little hot.

The other girl, who was slightly taller than the shero, had her lips pressed in a thin line. Braids encircled her brown head, making her look like an African princess. He'd learned her name was LaTisha.

LaTisha tapped the thumb of her right hand to

the tip of each finger. *Tap-tap-tap-tap.* Then she started again at her index finger. *Tap-tap-tap-tap.*

It was a tic Charlie had seen in the highest ranks of leadership, on down to some of the meanest prisoners of war. The repetitive motion was most often brought on by anxiety, either a need to control a situation or the fear that came with a loss of control.

Charlie wanted to sink down to his haunches and tell LaTisha that things were about to change. For the better. He wanted to tell Daria that he wasn't the villain in this story. He was the hero come to rescue them all.

He wouldn't have made it to the girls if he tried. Three boys stood in the path between Charlie and the girls. The three male foster kids all stood perfectly still with their arms crossed over their small chests as they frowned at him.

Denny, the skateboarding runaway, glared at Charlie with clear suspicion. Even after Charlie had given the kid a ride across town and didn't rat him out to Savy. Charlie understood that glare. He'd given it to Father Matthews when he'd come to him as a foster kid. Denny was clearly the big man on campus. Now that Charlie was on the scene, Denny's power was in question.

The boy standing next to Denny had been introduced to Charlie as Miguel. Miguel wore a shirt a size too small for his round belly and pants held up by a belt stretching against the last hole in the loop. Miguel tried to glare, though his gaze would dart away anytime Charlie tried to catch it.

The last child, who had cornrows like LaTisha, even though his hair was blond had Charlie's full attention. Ashton, or Ashtray as the boy had corrected, wore a Snoop Dog t-shirt and low-slung jeans with no belt. Charlie was a fan of hip hop himself—Wu Tang For Life. But there was a fine line between fandom and faking it, and Ashtray was on the wrong side of that line. Charlie would just have to have a heart-to-heart with the kid.

He'd have a heart-to-heart with all of the kids, just like his father had done with him and his brothers. By the end of the day, they would all be one big, happy family.

"Charlie?"

Charlie turned to the sound of Savy's voice. She beckoned him into the office of the foster home. Charlie followed her. He'd follow the woman anywhere. Luckily, with his father's solution, it would be Savy that would follow him home this time. She'd follow him home and stay forever.

It was time—finally time for their forever. After

all these years of waiting. After all the missed opportunities. It was here.

"We can't," she said the moment the door to the office was closed.

Charlie had been reaching for her, pulling her into his embrace and aiming his lips for her. "We can't what? I can't kiss you? We're going to be married."

"We're not getting married." Savy shoved at his chest. It was another of the ineffectual shoves, so Charlie held tight.

"Why not?" he said, tightening his embrace and resting his nose in the strands of her hair.

When no answer was forthcoming, Charlie peered down at the woman he loved. Savy tried to answer, but her lips only open and closed. No words came out. What did was a huge sigh that sounded like surrender.

"Charlie, this is crazy."

"What's crazy?" he asked as he nuzzled the space behind her ear. It was her soft spot and how he got her to agree to most things.

"I can't bring these kids to the ranch," she said after letting loose a shuddery breath.

"It's the perfect solution. I'm only sorry I didn't

think of it myself. There's plenty of space for each kid and the two of us."

They were so close. So close to finally having everything they both had dreamed of since they were kids in this room, hiding from the cruel realities of their world.

"This is it, Sav. This is our someday. Our start to forever. It's here."

Savy leaned into him. She rested her cheek against his chest, right where his heart beat for her. She tilted her head up until her nose was just under his chin. She exhaled, and Charlie felt the entire world stop.

"I came back for you," he said. "Let me take you home with me."

He'd been flying at top speeds for years. Always racing forward to get closer to her. The ride had been bumpy, but this was the smooth landing he'd always imagined.

A crash permeated the air with turbulence. The change in pressure forced Charlie and Savy apart. The disturbance of the children's voices rose until that was all that could be heard. Charlie took a step toward the door, but Savy held him back.

"I can't bring this pack of wild animals to Flying Cross," she said. "They'll destroy it."

"Flying Cross withstood the six of us," said Charlie. "A skater boy, Vanilla Ice, and that little daredevil you got out there won't stand a chance."

She cracked a smile at his characterizations of her kids. Savy's smile was everything. There was no way he was taking off in any direction without her. Never again.

Charlie wrapped her back up in his embrace. "They'll also have you and me. Together. We withstood the six Matthews boys and the three James sisters. We're unstoppable."

"Yeah," she grinned. "We do make a great team when it comes to wayward misfits."

"So, is that a yes?" he asked.

"A yes to moving in with you?"

"I'm not that kind of man. You'll need to make an honest Matthews out of me."

Savy snorted at that. Her laughter and amusement weren't enough. He wanted the right to be by her side forever. He wanted her to take his last name. He wanted to stand before his father and his God and proclaim this woman as his, and he as hers.

"I want to marry you, Sav. I'll take everything that comes with you. Say yes."

Savy closed her eyes. When she opened them,

Charlie knew he had the answer he wanted. He sank down to his knee.

"Savy James, will you marry me?"

"Yes, Charlie. Yes, I will."

The diamond ring was still on her finger. He pressed a kiss to it. Then he stood and pressed a kiss to her. The moment his lips met hers, another crash sounded, and the door banged open.

In the doorway stood the three little thugs who would now be Charlie's responsibility to guide. Each kid looked feral and ready for a fight. Charlie wasn't going to fight any of these kids. He knew what they needed. A firm hand to guide them on the right path. Luckily for them, he had both a firm hand, and he knew of a well-tread path.

"We're not moving to a farm."

"I'm scared of horses."

"This is slave labor. Not only is that against the law. It's bad behavior."

Oh, man. Someone needed to get little Ashtray a rhyming dictionary. Charlie's ears would be bleeding by the end of the week unless the kid came up with better verses.

"Ms. Savy," said Daria, the Daredevil, as she squeezed past the boys, "I don't want to move to a stable with horses. I want to sleep on a bed, not in hay."

"That," Daria pointed to the tall, wooden structure that loomed large in the afternoon sunlight, "is a barn."

Technically, she was right. The two-story wood structure was indeed a barn. Though Savy knew firsthand, there were no horses inside. She knew that there were six separate bedrooms, three on the bottom floor and three on the top floor. She also knew that the oak tree around the back led to the second-floor bedroom on the back right. Furthermore, she knew that same tree was sturdy enough to handle the weight of a young girl and young boy as they stole quiet moments away from prying eyes.

A small smile played at Savy's lips as she allowed those memories to swirl around her head along with the light breeze of the day. She caught sight of Charlie in the distance walking toward her. His gaze followed the trajectory of her eyes, and she knew he was remembering those stolen moments of their youth as well.

"You said we wouldn't be sleeping in a barn, Ms. Savy," said Daria.

"It's against code to put kids in a barn," said Denny.

"I like horses," said LaTisha. "I'd be okay sleeping on a horse."

"Oh, wait!" Daria's cape billowed in the wind as she whipped around. "Can I sleep on a horse? That would be totally different, especially if the horse was my animal familiar."

"You're not sleeping in a barn or with the horses," said Savy. "You'll each have your own bedroom, as per DFACS code."

Both Daria and LaTisha pouted. Denny narrowed his gaze, clearly looking around for something else to complain about. Miguel and Ashton maintained dubious expressions.

"But there are horses here, right?" said Daria. "The Amazonians rode horses in Themyscira. Diana rode one in *Wonder Woman 1984* when she was just a kid. Can I ride one, Ms. Savy, please? Please?"

"Didn't Diana fall off that horse?" said LaTisha.

Daria threw the older girl a scowl. "She did, but she got back on and nearly won the whole tournament against all the older women. You always have to get back up and try again. Right, Ms. Savy?"

"Yeah," said LaTisha. "But Diana lost the tournament because she took a shortcut. You can't win in life if you take shortcuts. Right, Ms. Savy?"

Savy had not been paying attention to the film. She'd been paying attention to the hottie Chris Pine who played Wonder Woman's back-from-the-dead-boyfriend, Steve Trevor. Steve was a pilot that had the same smolder in his eyes as Charlie.

Charlie was almost to her. Even from this distance, Savy could see the burning flame in his hazel eyes that brought out the gold flecks. Her Charlie, whose lips were raised in a smirk as he took her in. Savy had kissed that smirk yesterday. She would get to kiss it again today. Then tomorrow, and on and on for the rest of their lives because now—unlike poor dead Steve from the movie—Charlie was here to stay. Forever.

When he reached her, Charlie wrapped an arm around her waist and pulled her to him. His smiling lips pressed into Savy's temple, making her think thoughts that definitely were not PG rated. He pulled away, his eyes burning into hers, so bright she felt hot in the tank top she wore this afternoon.

"I'll teach you to ride," Charlie said when he turned to the kids. "But first, you have to learn how to take care of the horses."

"Will you teach me to shoot a bow and arrow from a horse?" asked Daria. "It would really help my superhero cred."

"Super heroine," corrected LaTisha.

"I can teach you to shoot a bow and arrow, too," said Charlie. "But not while on a horse. One thing at a time."

Ashton and LaTisha perked up at that. Miguel looked horrified. Daria looked up at Charlie as if he were Superman in the flesh.

Denny took one look at his sister's clear admiration. Then he turned to Charlie. Charlie grinned at Denny. Denny's gaze narrowed, just as Christopher Reeve's did when he shot lasers from his eyes. Being that Charlie had never been interested in superheroes, the kid's death glare skated right by him.

Savy wasn't so sure about the list of activities Charlie had planned. She encouraged more academic and artistic activities. She was a proponent of physical activities, but more along the lines of bowling with the kiddie guard rail up.

"It smells like horse sh—"

Both Savy and Charlie turned glares on Denny. They might not be on the same page activity-wise, but they were in synch when it came to language and manners.

"Get used to that smell," said Charlie. "One of your chores will be to shovel it."

"So we're slave labor," said Denny.

"Slaves didn't have a choice," said Savy. "You do. You either live here in warmth and comfort, with three square meals, with people who care about you, and you do your chores. Or you get put back into the system where you roll the dice on the next home you end up in."

Denny glanced at his sister. They all knew that that roll of dice would almost certainly mean they'd be pulled apart.

"I'll shovel for you, Denny," said Daria in a whisper loud enough for everyone to hear. "I'll use my super strength."

Daria wrapped a spindly arm around her brother. Her cape flapped at Denny's knees in the light breeze. Her older brother's glare softened for just a second as he peered down at her.

"You look super strong," said Charlie. "Why don't

you come meet my favorite horse. I think he'll like you."

Daria dropped the arm she had around her brother. The edge of her cape lifted as she reached for Charlie's hand. Denny's hands tightened into fists as he watched the two walk off.

LaTisha grabbed at Charlie's other hand. Ashton took ginger steps in the dirt as though any speck would end up on his polished sneakers. He pulled his cap low on the cornrows Foxy had braided into his hair this morning. Miguel hung back alongside Denny.

Savy knew the young boy wasn't standing in solidarity with Denny. Miguel was not a fan of any creature on four legs, be they horses or mice or anything in between. Denny and Miguel were temporary allies.

Most foster kids didn't believe in permanency, especially when it came to adults. How could they when their own parents weren't in their lives to stick up for them? To complicate matters more, a series of strangers all insisted they had the children's backs. Those adults were often on a conveyor belt that never stopped until the kids were legal.

Savy knew all of this firsthand. Her own parents had been in and out of her life since she was Daria's age. By the time she'd reached Denny's age, she knew better than to depend on her mother. Or any adult, for that matter.

Denny and Daria had been with her for months, but they both still lived out of their backpacks, ready at any moment to leave and be moved away. Savy needed them to understand that she wasn't about to let them go. The truth was, she couldn't make that promise. Not when she was at the mercy of the state, just as they were.

"Denny, this is a good thing. I promise you're going to like it here if you give it a chance."

Denny shrugged. "I've only got four more years before I'm eighteen and can get me and my sister out of this. I can hold my nose for that long. Or however long you stick around."

"Great job, Daria. You're a regular Amazonian."

The girl in the cape preened at Charlie as she bounced atop the horse like they were on a Merry Go Round. Her spindly legs tried to kick the horse like she was a jockey in a race. Luckily, Duff was the most docile horse on the ranch and ignored her antics as he walked on with his energetic charge.

That was now, but back when Charlie was a rough and tumble adolescent, Duff had been known to pull on the lead and buck at the slightest provocation. Charlie and his brothers had provided a lot of provocation. Mainly with each other. Though the horses had sensed the turbulence within them, too. Back then, when they were all young and easily riled up, Duff would pin his ears to his head whenever one of them came near in a clear sign of agitation. His eyes would widen, and his nostrils would flare in nervous anxiety.

It was a wonder that none of the Matthews boys had gotten a hoof in their bellies or broken their necks from being thrown. Just as the wild stallion had had to go through his paces with the young humans, the boys had had a lot of lessons to learn from the animals, from the work on the farm, from their foster parents who had had the patience of saints as they worked with the six wild animals they'd brought into their home. In comparison to his brothers, these five kids would be a walk in the park.

"Faster, Mr. Charlie. Faster."

Charlie continued his slow strides, leading Duff around the pen in a leisurely walk. The horse's eyes were half-closed as Daria bounced in the saddle. The aged stallion likely couldn't even feel the girl's slight weight.

"Not yet," said Charlie. "You gotta learn to walk before you can fly, Wonder Woman."

"Wonder Person," called LaTisha from her place, sitting on the fence. "Heroes should be non-binary."

"Right," said Charlie, not truly understanding what that meant. But he couldn't let a ten-year-old see that she knew something he didn't.

The kids had finished all of the chores he'd set out for them today. That had mainly been learning to muck out the stalls and organizing the tack walls. They'd done a fair job of it. Even Miguel, who had stayed at the stall closest to the exit. He'd perked up a bit when he got to help place down new hay and water for the horses. The kid liked helping with how the food went in, not how it came out.

The oldest kid, Denny, had made a mess of the mess left by the horses. Then the delinquent screwed his features into a helpless pout and let the pitchfork clatter to the ground.

It was the old screw up the chore so that the adult won't ask you to do it again tactic. Charlie had tried the same tactic when he was young. Father Matthews had simply nodded his head as though in commiseration. Then he'd shrugged and said, *Try again*. When Charlie had proceeded to make an even bigger mess, he was met with the same result from his foster father. By the time Charlie learned his lesson, it was the dead of night and his dinner was cold.

Denny was still learning that lesson while the

younger kids were reaping their reward of riding one of the horses they'd just cared for. By the time Denny came out of the stall with sweat beading his brow, the others had already gone off to explore the ranch before dinner.

"Do I need to triple check your work, son?" Charlie asked.

Denny's jaw ticked. Charlie was almost certain it had nothing to do with checking behind the kid. The first time Father Matthews had called him *son*, Charlie had balked, too. Until he'd come to love the endearment.

"You know slave labor is against foster care rules," said Denny. "I could have you reported."

Charlie had said the exact same thing to Father Matthews. Yeah, he and this kid were on the road to a sappy After School Special happy ending real soon.

"These are chores, Denny. We all do them as a family to keep this place running."

The baby fat that still clung to the kid's cheeks hardened. He bit at his lip as though trying to hold his tongue. At his sides, his fists clenched.

Yeah, this was definitely a moment for wise words that would open the kid's heart and bring him closer to Charlie's side. Only a step or two closer, though. Charlie estimated it would take him a good couple of months before he won the kid over completely.

"We're going to learn to work together as a team, as a family. This is your home now, for as long as you want it to be."

Something sparked in the kid's eyes. Not like a fire that burned off hard edges. More like a light coming on in a dark room.

"You know what, Charlie—"

"It's Mr. Charlie, to you."

"I might've judged you too harshly." Denny pressed his lips together, then opened them to let out a sigh. "I'm not used to people believing in me."

Maybe Charlie would have to revise his heart melting estimate. Looked like that Afterschool Special ending would happen sooner rather than later.

"Truce?" Denny opened his arms.

Charlie wasn't certain of protocol. Was he allowed to give a foster kid a hug? He certainly didn't want to reject the kid now that he was making some leeway.

In the end, Charlie decided to throw caution to

the wind. They were standing out in a wide-open field. He wrapped his arms around the kid's back. Denny was nothing but skin and bones. That would all change soon as he worked the fields alongside Charlie.

"Thank you for this chance, Mr. Charlie," said Denny. He mimicked Charlie's motions, patting him on the back.

Charlie watched Denny walk off toward the barn house. Visions of teaching the kid catch and advising him about girls flitted through Charlie's mind. He'd always known he wanted to be a father. He knew he'd be good at it, too, with the example Father Matthews had set. Now he would get his chance sooner than later.

With a pep in his own step, Charlie went in search of his fiancée. He found her standing in one of the bedrooms of the guest house, looking at the made-up bed. Charlie scooped Savy into his arms from behind.

"Hurry, Joe. We don't have much time. Charlie will be back any second."

Charlie squeezed Savy until she giggled uncontrollably. "Trying to incite fratricide?"

"Yeah, I'm still mad at your brother for eating all the Jolly Ranchers that one Halloween."

"That was over fifteen years ago."

She turned in his arms, grinning up at him. "I still can't believe this is really happening."

"It is, Savy. It's happening. I'm going to marry you."

"I'm gonna marry you right back."

He dipped his head to hers. Her lips were sweeter than all the Halloween candy he'd ever had all put together. Charlie would never tire of kissing this woman, and now he could do it year-round instead of stealing moments while he was home for a holiday.

"Will you two get a room," said Foxy from the doorway.

"This is my room," said Savy.

"Not for long," said Foxy as she headed into the second bedroom. "Joe's coming home in a couple of days."

Charlie frowned at that prediction. As far as he knew, Joe was still in the thick of boring military legalese in his role as a Judge Advocate General or JAG. But he knew Foxy's foresight had a fifty-fifty chance of being right as being wrong.

"Great," Savy sighed dramatically. "So now I'll have to juggle two brothers."

Charlie ignored the love of his life's antics. Mainly

because he knew his younger brother had always had a crush on Foxy. A crush Foxy had always been oblivious to, even though she claimed to be psychic.

"Wait a minute?" Savy tried to pull away from Charlie, but he didn't let her go. "If you're here, and Foxy's here, who's minding the kids?"

"I let them roam."

Savy's pull became a jerk. It was no matter. Charlie still held her tight to him.

"You let five city kids roam on a ranch?"

"City kids?" Charlie scoffed. "They lived at Bright Horizons, which was surrounded by forests and wildlife. They're fine. I told them to keep the ranch house in view and not to go to the Silvers because those women eat little children."

"Charlie," Savy sighed in exasperation. "Who knows what trouble they'll get into?"

"Sav, relax. I'm making great headway with them. Denny even gave me a hug."

Savy went slack in his arms. Her jaw tensed as her gaze widened. "Denny hugged you?"

"Yeah." Charlie grinned, entirely pleased with himself and his progress. Though he wondered why Savy wasn't singing his praises? Instead, she patted down his pockets. "What are you doing?"

"Did you have your phone on you during this *hug*?" She said *hug* as though she were making finger air quotes around the word. As though the word *hug* didn't at all mean what it should mean.

"Yeah, it's..." Charlie patted down his back pocket. His empty back pocket. "That little... I can't believe I just got taken by a fourteen-year-old punk. I have real-world experience leading troops into danger zones. Heck, I have years of combat from living with my brothers."

Charlie turned on his heel, marching toward the door. Before he got to the handle, a knock sounded from the other side. Charlie pulled it open to find Denny standing there.

"I think you dropped these, Mr. Charlie." The kid held up his phone and wallet.

Charlie shuffled back a step. He tipped his head to the side as he regarded the kid. Denny could've taken his phone and wallet and wreaked a bit of havoc with them. Instead, here he was, handing the lost items back to Charlie.

Oh, yeah. He definitely was getting through to this kid.

Charlie wanted to go in for another hug. The kid deserved it with all the progress he'd made today.

But that might be way too touchy-feely. So instead, he held out his hand.

"Thanks, Denny."

"Sure thing."

Denny gave Charlie's hand a shake. It was a little weak, but they'd work on that later. A man's first impression was in his handshake.

"Good talk earlier."

"Glad you think so, son."

Denny's eye twitched. But it was almost imperceptible. They'd work on that too. The kid nodded and turned on his heel.

"See that?" Charlie said to Savy, who stood watching the interaction from over his shoulder. "I'm getting to him."

"I don't know." Savy scrunched her nose and sucked at her teeth. "He's up to something."

"If he is, he won't outsmart us. Not the dynamic duo."

Savy opened her mouth to say more, but Charlie silenced her with a kiss. The shock of her sweetness never got old. It never would. The two of them were forces to be reckoned with apart. Together, they would be unstoppable. Especially when faced with a fourteen-year-old kid who simply wanted to belong.

Charlie would teach Denny that, too. He'd teach

them all about the joy of belonging not just to someone but to a family.

"Hey," he said when he broke the kiss. "I'm going to marry you."

"So I heard." She grinned up at him before bringing his head down to hers for even more kisses.

12

———

Savy felt a tickle move up her calf. She bit her lip but was unable to hide the giggle that escaped her mouth. She was too old to be playing footsie. But here she was seated at the Matthews's dinner table, tangling her bare feet with Charlie Matthews's boot.

Charlie was the only horseman she knew in town who'd never taken to cowboy boots. Even at a young age, Charlie had known he was going into the military to follow in Father Matthews's footsteps. So it was Charlie's combat boot that snaked around Savy's ankle to lift up her heel and rest her instep on his laces.

"I see someone wasn't playing around this afternoon," said Father Matthews.

Charlie's foot landed with a thud on the floor. Savy snapped her foot back under her own chair. When they looked up, the older man wasn't looking at either of them.

"This looks delightful, Miguel," said Father Matthews. "You truly know your way around a kitchen."

"It's fusion," said Miguel as he served up the steaming dish that smelled of onion and tomatoes and peppers.

Instead of tortillas, there were mashed potatoes beneath the salsa. The dish should not have worked. The watering of Savy's mouth and the grumbling of her belly reminded her how well the Midwest potatoes and the Mexican dishes fused.

"Miguel is going to be a chef when he grows up," said Foxy.

"I'm working on my knife skills," said Miguel as he placed a bowl of shredded cheese at the center of the table. "You'll notice how the cut of the onion and peppers are uniform because I julienned them. That's different from dicing, which is when you make them smaller and more square than rectangle."

"You should set another plate," said Foxy. "We're missing someone."

Savy's heart gave a little jump as she looked around the table. But all five children were accounted for. Sometimes her sister made predictions that came true. Sometimes, Foxy just said things that made no sense.

"I don't like vegetables," said Daria.

"You won't know they're there because they're so small," said Savy.

"Miguel just told me they're there." Daria turned to Father Matthews. "Vegetables are my kryptonite."

Father Matthews nodded sagely. "That's too bad. Spinach is what made my childhood hero Popeye, The Sailorman, grow strong."

"Who's Popeye? Was he your father? Are you going to be my grandpa?"

Father Matthews smiled indulgently at the child. Savy couldn't take her eyes off that smile. She'd often imagined him smiling at her like that when she became his daughter. That hadn't happened when she was just a little girl. He and his wife had only picked the boys from the foster home to come and live with them.

Father Matthews had never been anything but kind to her and her sisters. His wife, too, when she'd been alive. Tessa Matthews had been something out of a Disney fairy godmother lineup, the guardian angel every child would've loved having at their back.

Savy had told the woman that she would be marrying her son when she was just twelve years old. But then her own mother had swept in and carried Savy and her sisters away again. By the time Savy was able to come back to the Flying Cross Ranch, Tessa Matthews had flown up to be with the other angels.

Back here on earth, Tessa's husband still kept Savy at a distance. Which was confusing to Savy because he knew—everyone knew—that she was head over heels in love with his son. The same son who was back to rubbing his booted calf against hers and grinning at her from across the table.

Charlie had that look in his eyes. That look that told her she was going to be kissed senseless the moment he got her alone. Under the heat of that smolder, Savy forgot about the older Matthews and focused exclusively on the younger man.

"Who would like to say grace?" asked Father Matthews.

All around the square table, the five children looked up in confusion. Forks were in hands. Mouths were open, ready to shovel in Miguel's fusion feast. Gazes were wide as they tried to decipher this foreign word.

"We didn't say grace at the foster home," said Savy. "The children often came from different religious and cultural backgrounds. So I thought it best that each child practice the customs they were taught, or that they gravitated toward."

When she looked across the table, she noted that Charlie winced.

Father Matthews pursed his lips. He didn't frown. The man never frowned, but it was clear that he wasn't pleased with her chosen protocol.

"It's not that I don't believe in a higher power," Savy tried to backtrack. "I just think that children should find their own path to the Creator."

"Or Creatress," said LaTisha.

"How will you know the path to the Creator-" Father Matthews offered the child a glowing smile. "Or Creatress, if you don't have a guide?"

The kids all turned their gazes to Savy. The forks squeezed in their hands, which still hovered over the bounty before them.

Savy pasted on the smile she gave government officials, hospital staff, and public school teachers when they questioned her methods. "Children are born smart. We have to let them make mistakes so that they can grow up."

Father Matthews nodded. He didn't verbally disagree with her, but his smile faded at the corners.

"I'll say grace," said Charlie. "The kids can listen and determine if it resonates with them."

Charlie offered his father a placating smile. He offered Savy a wink.

Savy was grateful for Charlie's interference. She didn't want to offend Father Matthews. Not when he'd opened up his home to the lot of them. Not when she wanted his blessing to marry his son. Not when she still craved the fatherly affection she'd never gotten from him.

"Father God, we thank you for—"

"Why did you say Father God?" asked LaTisha. "It makes most sense to me that God is a woman. It's women that give birth. Not men."

Inwardly, Savy wanted to give the little girl a high five for the logical question. This is what happened when adults let kids think for themselves instead of telling them what to think.

"Is love male or female?" Father Matthews asked in his patient voice.

LaTisha screwed her button nose to think this over. "I don't think love is a person."

"But you can feel it? Can't you?"

LaTisha nodded slowly.

"Love isn't something you can prove. You can only feel it. Doesn't matter if you're loved by a male or a female. When you're loved, you're simply loved. God is love."

There was a peaceful hum hovering in the room at this pronouncement. Each child looked at Father Matthews with thoughtful gazes. Even Savy felt her heart expand at the explanation.

"I'm hungry," Daria said into the quiet moment. "Dear God, can we just eat already?"

"Amen," said Denny.

Forks dug into plates. Lips smacked in appreciation. Savy's own fork was only an inch from her mouth when the doorbell rang. She looked up at Foxy, who shrugged as if to say, *I told you so.*

When Father Matthews made a motion to rise, Savy held out her hand to stop him. "I'll get it," she said, rising from her chair.

She took one glance at the fragrant, steaming plate of food before heading into the main room. When she opened the door, she found an unwanted visitor there. She'd curse her sister for not warning her about exactly who this guest was.

"Are you here to see Father Matthews?" asked

Savy. Although she knew that couldn't be the case. Not when Tina Billings wasn't here in her nurse's scrubs. Instead, she was standing in a slinky black dress that looked like it would slip off her with a slight wind.

"No," Tina smirked. "I have a date with Charlie."

Savy slow blinked. Then her eyelids fluttered in quick succession. She'd expected something along those lines with how the woman was dressed. Still, it was a shock to actually hear her gumption.

Really? Was dating so hard in Honor Valley that a woman had to show up on the doorstep of an engaged man? A man who'd been engaged since he was a kid.

"He texted me to pick him up here."

Tina held up her cellphone. Savy barely glanced at it. But in the flash that she saw, the sequence of numbers was familiar to her. Those were Charlie's digits. In exactly the order that would ring his phone.

But no. That couldn't be right. Charlie had never been on a date that didn't include her. Putting that most important fact aside, Charlie would never ask a girl to pick him up. He was far too much of a gentleman not to pick a woman up at her place. The most wrong thing about this whole scenario was the text. Charlie hated typing with his thumbs.

Savy stepped aside to let Tina in. Really, it was the only decent thing to do. It was chilly in the air tonight, and the woman was barely dressed.

Tina didn't wait for a formal invitation. She walked into the house like she owned the place. Either she followed her nose to the dining room, or she had acute senses that were tuned into bachelors.

"Who's this?" asked Charlie when the two women appeared in the dining room.

"Your date," said Savy.

"My what?" Charlie's fork clattered down to his now empty plate.

Savy took one more look at her cooling dinner before she turned to the culprit in this scenario. If she weren't so hungry, she might've found the whole deal a little funny. But her stomach was grumbling, so she was cranky when she said, "Let's ask Denny."

13

———

Charlie shut Tina's car door with a decisive thunk. The naughty nurse in a scrub of a dress gave him one last pouty look before putting the car into reverse and heading down the driveway.

With that bit of business done, Charlie engaged the locking feature on his cell phone. That was a first. He spent a few minutes pressing his thumb to the device, ensuring that only he would have access to it from now on. Then he crumpled the small piece of paper with Tina's number on it that he'd completely forgotten was in his wallet.

He let the scrap flit out of his hand on the night's breeze. It bumped along the hay strewn over the ground. Charlie didn't consider tossing the refuse as littering, not when the horses would likely eat it in the morning. That is, if a night critter didn't grab it to use in its bedding.

He didn't care what became of it. It hadn't caused him any trouble, just a slight annoyance that he'd had to get up from the dinner table before being served seconds. By the sassy look Savy had given him when she'd picked up her knife and fork, he knew there wouldn't be anything left of Miguel's dish when he came back inside.

Turning, Charlie was met with a youthful face full of defiance. Pinched cheeks that couldn't pull off a hallowed look because of the lingering baby fat. Spindly arms crossed over a chest that would barrel out in a few years. Scowling eyes filled with mistrust and wariness.

Man, that had been him a decade ago. So ready to defy any type of authority, no matter if it hurt him in the process. After a slew of foster homes, it was only Father Matthews that had gotten through Charlie's distrust of the world. The man had done that without raising his voice in anger.

"So, you're trying to get rid of me," Charlie said calmly in his best imitation of his adoptive father.

"Very good, Sherlock." Denny's head cocked to the side as he glared at Charlie.

"You know, I tried that with every foster parent I came in contact with when I was your age."

"Bet that was easy. Them getting rid of you, I mean. Easy to get lost in dinosaur caves."

"Funny. You're funny." Charlie bent down so that he was eye level with the kid. Hazel eyes, like his own, stared back at him, unflinching. That was fine because Charlie didn't flinch either. This next part was the most important part for this kid to understand. "Here's what you need to know about me, Denny. I will never, ever, leave that woman."

Denny glanced down the road where Nurse Tina's car was now out of sight. However, the kid seemed to think better of whatever crack he was about to make that put Charlie with the other woman. A mischievous glint lit up the golden flecks of his eyes.

"Really?" Denny smirked. "Because I've been with Savy for months, and I've never seen or heard of you."

"I've been in the Air Force." Charlie straightened to his full height. "And it's Ms. Savy to you."

"Not Mrs. Matthews, because as a pilot, you don't walk away. You fly away. Got it."

"Look here, you little—"

Charlie had taken a step toward the kid. He

stopped abruptly. Not only had he raised his voice, he felt anger coursing through him.

For his part, Denny smirked again. The look on the little demon spawn's face hollered, *gotcha*.

The little cretin had gotten Charlie. Denny had gotten him. And now Denny was stuck with him.

Because Charlie saw it. Charlie saw behind that raised chin and those red cheeks. Charlie saw the kid in those eyes that had seen too much. That crooked grin that was a twitch away from wobbling in a sob. Those balled fists that had had to defend himself when there was no adult around to do it for him.

Charlie saw it all. Because Charlie had lived every second of it himself. But he'd forgotten.

He'd been so long inside a home where he didn't have to guard against anything but his brothers' good-natured roughhousing. He'd been so long on a team that would lift his head for him at any disappointment. He'd been so long standing back-to-back alongside men who would throw a punch at anyone who dared raise a fist to him.

Charlie had started this life on empty. Now, his cup overflowed. Not just from his family but from the love of his life.

When he'd left the Air Force, all he could think

about was getting back here to Savy. To finally start their lives together. She had left her singing career years ago to answer the call to the foster care system, to save kids like them.

There was a ringing in Charlie's ears. Much like when he was at high altitudes. Looking down at Denny, Charlie realized he was being called. Not just to a life with Savy. He was being called to save these kids.

"Crap," he sighed.

"Excellent language to use in front of a minor, Captain," said the smart-mouthed minor.

"I'm not gonna be as good at this as Savy."

"Could've fooled me."

Charlie ignored Denny as the realizations kept rolling in. "I'm not gonna be as good as my father, either. You and I are going to butt heads. We're probably not going to get along for a while. You already don't like me. I'm trying hard to warm to you."

It wasn't the most ooey-gooey as motivational speeches went. But Charlie wasn't an Afterschool Special. He wasn't a Disney Prince. He wasn't even sure if he qualified for the Hallmark Channel?

But he was real.

He'd grown up around boys. Rough boys that didn't talk about their feelings. He still wasn't sure his brother, Topher, had actual feelings? What the Matthews boys did do was tell the truth, work hard, and take care of family.

"The other thing you need to know about me is that I don't give up. Ever. I waited my whole life to be with that woman. I love her. She loves you. And so, we are going to get along."

Charlie didn't know what he expected from the kid. A tear at the corner of his eye before he broke down and admitted all he'd ever wanted was to be loved. A sigh of resignation before he flung his arms wide open and clung to Charlie. Whatever Charlie expected was mute because what he got was a snort.

"Whatever, man. I'll be outta here in a couple years."

"That's true," Charlie agreed. And that should've been the end of it. They could simply tolerate each other for a few years. "Or this could be your home base, a place you can always come back to no matter how old you are or how far you go."

Denny took a step back. Then another. His arms were now straight down at his sides, hands locked into fists. Clearly, Charlie was not breaking through the kid's defenses. But he wasn't ready to give up. The whistling of the night's wind was far too close to a harp melody that would be played during a family sitcom at the time after the kid finally owned up to their mistake and the lovable, dopey dad got down on one knee to impart the life lesson for that week.

Charlie didn't get down on one knee, but he did take a step closer to the kid. "I came from Bright Horizons too. Father Matthews took me and my brothers in. We all made something of ourselves. You could do it on your own, but it's easier to do it with a family."

"I don't see anyone else around here."

"Not yet. Not now. But we always come back. Because this is my forever home. It can be your forever home, too. For you and your sister."

That got a response out of him. That tough veneer slipped for just a quick second at the mention of Daria.

"There's no guarantee you'll stay together outside of here. If you decide to stay here, no one will ever take you from this place. I promise."

Charlie held out his hand. Palm up. He waited a full sixty seconds while Denny mulled the offer over. Finally, a limp hand barely touched his.

"I'm not calling you dad."

Charlie perked up at the word dad. He let it go the second Denny dropped his hand. It was a start. And Charlie planned for them to go the distance.

14

"Good work today, Super Daria." Savy gave Daria's cape a shake. The piece of cloth was filthy. But Savy knew better than to secret it away for a wash while the girl was still awake. She'd have to sneak back in the middle of the night to run it through the wash. And just like always, when the kid woke up, she'd believe her pristine cape came to her by way of magic.

"That's a pretty lame superhero name, Ms. Savy," said Daria. "For one, it reveals my secret identity."

"Ah, good point." Savy came and sat on the edge of the bed. The quilt was hand sewn, likely the work of Tessa Matthews. Charlie had shown Savy the quilt his foster mother had made for him when he'd first come to Flying Cross Ranch. She'd made each of her boys one to keep him warm at night.

"You can give me a hug if you want," Daria said.

There was faux annoyance in her tone. Many foster kids weren't used to, or interested in, physical forms of affection. Especially those that were abandoned by their birth parents. Many kids in the system were never hugged by their parents or shown any affection. It often took weeks, or even months, for them to stand any form of care, be it verbal or physical.

Savy always trod very carefully in this part of her work. She'd found the best tactic was to make affection a choice that the child was in charge of. "Are you sure it's okay? I know it's been a physically demanding day for you and your powers."

"No, it's fine. I have a little bit of energy left. And you did a good job today, so you probably need a hug."

Daria opened her arms. Savy leaned down and scooped the girl's small body into her chest. She wanted to squeeze tightly, to show Daria how much she cared. She wanted her to know that her love was real and lasting. But she couldn't make those kinds of promises as a foster parent.

Any of these kids could be taken from her at any

moment. Which was why Savy worked so hard to keep her reputation as a foster parent pristine. She knew no one else would love these kids like she did.

"Did you know that Clark Kent grew up on a farm?" Daria asked as she snuggled deep into the quilt. "So did Captain Kirk and Luke Skywalker. I think this place will be good for my backstory."

Savy grinned down at the little imp. This place would be good for Daria to grow big and strong. It'd be good for Miguel to learn about fresh foods and how they're grown. LaTisha would find a ton of reading nooks out here in the woods. Unfortunately, the ranch would completely ruin Ashton's street cred, being that there were no paved streets or corners he could hang on to try to become a rap star.

Denny was the one Savy worried about. But she had faith in Charlie. If anyone could turn that kid around, it would be him.

The two males were so much alike.

Which meant they would butt heads before they would ever hug it out.

But together, she and Charlie would save that kid from himself, just like they saved each other.

She and Charlie. Savy couldn't believe that sentence was finally here in reality. She and Charlie were going to raise these kids together. She and

Charlie were going to get married. She and Charlie were finally starting their forever. Her dream had come true.

Peeking into each room of the bunkhouse, Savy saw that her kids were all tucked safely in bed. Each beneath one of Tessa's quilts. All lost in dreams of their own.

A sense of peace washed over Savy as she stepped out into the cool night breeze. The air smelled different on the ranch, cleaner even though she was surrounded by farm animals heeding the call to nature. This was now her home. This was now her life.

The creaking of wood against wood brought Savy's attention round to the big house. Father Matthews sat on the porch, rocking idly back and forth in an aged rocking chair. The moon kissed his weathered skin, making him look like a wise old man from epic fantasy lore.

"Long day?" he asked when Savy reached the porch.

"It was actually pretty peaceful. No one had to go to the hospital."

The old man chuckled. His eyes reflecting some of the moon's glow as though that celestial body was radiating from within him. Savy wouldn't have trouble believing that to be true. The Matthews boys all believed wholeheartedly that their father had a direct line to the Man Upstairs.

"You've done a good job with those kids," said Father Matthews. "You were gifted with the voice of an angel, but I believe you were born for this kind of work."

Savy leaned against the railing and looked out at the ranch. The land teemed with life, but all was silent now at this moment. "I didn't thank you personally for what you've done for us."

"It was purely selfish on my part," he said. "It's been too quiet here all these years."

Savy knew that wasn't entirely true. Father Matthews lived next door to a gaggle of Silvers. Those girls were just as much of a handful as the Matthews. Even before General Silver had passed away, the Silvers had always come to their neighbor for advice, problem-solving, and peacekeeping amongst them. Between the Matthews boys, the Silver sisters, and a few visits from the James girls, the Flying Cross Ranch was never quiet.

"You've already paid your dues raising your six boys," she said.

"Parenting never stops," he grinned, "meaning that bill is always accruing."

"For those kids in there," Savy inclined her head toward the bunkhouse, "parenting never started."

It had never started for her, either. She and her sisters were either an inconvenience to their mother, who wanted to be on the stage. Or they were a temporary act when she needed backup singers. Savy often wondered who she would've been if she'd been parented full time by Tessa and Haran Matthews.

"You are exactly the parent they need. I don't think I've ever told you personally how proud I am of the woman you've become."

The corners of Savy's eyes burned. She wasn't a crier. Tears were dangerous in the foster system. But she wasn't in a foster home any longer. She was in the safest place on earth. So when Haran Matthews opened his arms to her, Savy and her tears didn't hesitate to fall into him.

Savy had always dreamed of the Matthews adopting her and her sisters. But her mother would never terminate her parental rights. After each one of her slip-ups, as she called them, the state would take her girls. She would do just enough to keep the tether strings tight.

It wasn't until Fanny James overdosed when Foxy was nineteen that the strings had been permanently severed. By then, Savy had gained custody of both her sisters and was grinding hard to keep a roof over their heads and food in their bellies. Father Matthews helped out as much as she would allow him to. Money wasn't hard to come by. But funds weren't what Savy was starving for.

Father Matthews squeezed her tight. He pressed his palm into her spine, and she swore it flipped a switch, turning her from a strong, superwoman with a stiff upper lip to a little girl lost in need of saving. Savy clung to the warmth that radiated from his heart. She filled her nostrils with the familiar, comforting, earthy scent of him.

"Like I said, purely selfish motives."

With another press of his palm, the switch flipped again. Savy felt like a gas tank being filled to the brim. Not the regular unleaded fuel either. She had super diesel in her veins. By the time she pulled away from Father Matthews, she felt charged and ready to take on the world.

"Really? My own father is moving in on my girl?"

Charlie stood eying them from the porch steps. Moonlight bounced off his dark hair. The rays caught in his hazel eyes, making them sparkle. Savy took the few steps to the bottom of the porch to land in his arms.

She was overflowing with affection, and warmth, and energy, and love. She never imagined she could be this happy. But here she was, in the home she'd dreamed of living in as a girl, with the man she'd dreamed of every night.

Distantly, she heard Father Matthews excuse himself and head into the house. Savy sank into Charlie's arms. Neither said anything. They just held onto each other under the moonlight.

"They're a handful," he said, finally.

"You want out?"

His hold tightened around her. "I want you."

"Me and the kids are a packaged deal."

"So were you and your sisters. If Tricksy didn't scare me away, nothing will."

Savy pulled back to look at him. "We're really doing this?"

Charlie brushed a strand of hair across her temple and tucked it back behind her ear. "We're really doing this."

They were really doing this. Savy waited for surprise to wash over her. It never came. Instead, the peace of the night rang quietly in her ears... until a shout rang out in the night.

Charlie jerked away from her. His feet were

already in motion toward the bunkhouse. Savy tugged on his arm, holding him back.

"Nope, let them figure it out," said Savy.

"They sound like they're going to kill each other."

"If they do, then we won't have to settle the argument." Savy shrugged, wrapping her arms around his neck.

He chuckled, pressing his hand into the small of her back. "You sound exactly like Mother Matthews."

Savy's breath caught at the comparison. As silence once again washed over the night, that sense of rightness settled around her. All the parts of her life were coming together, like a quilt made just for her.

15

––––––

*C*harlie rolled over in his bed. He reached his hand out, but there were no warm curves to greet him. No sweet-scented hair to burrow his nose into. No heated flesh to brush his lips against.

Because Savy was not yet his wife. So, she was not allowed in his bed. A rule his father put his foot down on. Instead of holding onto Savy in real life, Charlie had spent the night dreaming of her.

Waking up was the last thing Charlie wanted to do this morning. Not when his dream was so good. He'd run his hands through his dream girl's thick curls. His vision of love had pressed her palms against his chest. All night long, he'd drowned in the smokey-sweetness that was his fantasy.

Charlie's heart raced even as the dream faded into the bright light of the morning. His body felt tasked, like he had spent the night holding tight to the woman who was his entire world. His lips felt bruised, like he had actually tussled with Savy's mouth into the wee hours. His arms felt heavy, like they had been locked around her form, fulfilling his promise of never letting her go.

His arms were empty now as he cracked one lid open. With the rays of the new day prying his eyes open, a thought ran through his head. It was that thought that yanked him out of sleep and into alert wakefulness.

In this shiny new day, Charlie could, in fact, spend his time with his arms wrapped tight around Savy. He could laze the day, exploring the fullness of her mouth. He could get lost in the curls of her hair.

What was he doing still in bed when the woman of his adolescent, teenage, and adult fantasies was just on the other side of the fence? He could be at the guest house in under five minutes if—

The sound of something tumbling down in his closet brought Charlie up to a sitting position. Someone was in there. If he had any doubts after the small thud of something falling, he knew it for certain by the gasp. That was a person, not a thing, that made that sound.

Was it Savy? Had she beaten him to a tryst? Was she defying Father Matthews's no fraternization until they'd put a ring on it edict? His naughty dream girl.

Charlie tossed off the sheets. The cool morning breeze hit his bare chest. He padded on bare feet to his closet. When he pulled the closet door open, he wasn't met with the tall, shapely love of his life. Instead, there was a short, gangly little girl in a cape and ill-fitting mask.

"Daria?"

The little girl sighed dramatically, looking entirely put out by Charlie's discovery of her. "I'm not Daria. She's a child. I'm Ultra Girl, a superhero on a secret mission."

"A secret mission in my closet?"

"I'm not stealing anything. Superheroes aren't thieves." She held up her hands, palms open. Only her palms weren't empty.

Daria stood to her full four-foot height, closing her hands and putting them on her not-yet-there hips. Her right hand balled into a fist to conceal what rested in her palm.

"Hand it over." Charlie held out his hand in a silent demand.

"I was just looking at it. I wasn't going to take it."

Daria opened her hand again to reveal a bronze medal hanging from a chain. The medal was in the shape of a cross. Instead of T-shapes, the ends of the cross were rounded like the blades of an airplane. Behind the blades were sharper blades jutting outward, like the rays of the sun.

"LaTisha looked you up on the internet," Daria said, stepping past him and out of the closet. "It said you were a hero and that you won a medal. Is this it?"

Charlie had been awarded the Flying Cross medal two years ago for an act of heroism during flight. The medal felt heavy in his palm now. Stepping away from the closet, he pulled out the chair at his old desk and slumped down into it.

Daria leaned on his thigh. She unfurled his fingers from around the medal so that it lay flat in his palm. Her round face peered down at it in awe.

"Did you get the bad guys?" she asked. "Is that why they gave you this?"

"Being a hero isn't always about getting the bad guys. I got this," he held the medal between his thumb and index finger, "because I saved some of the good guys."

The pink tip of Daria's tongue sneaked out of her mouth as she peered at the medal. Her eyes were big in her small face, as though she was transfixed by the medallion. "I want to be a superhero when I grow up."

"Soldiers are superheroes."

"Can girls be soldiers?"

"Of course," said Charlie. "Some of the best soldiers I know are women."

"Do soldiers ride horses?"

"Some do. I was a pilot, so I got to fly."

She considered that. Then she reached behind her head and undid the tie holding her flimsy mask in place.

"Oh!" Charlie widened his eyes and opened his mouth into a rounded O. "It's you, Daria. I had no clue you were Ultra Girl."

Daria giggled. "I decided I could let you in on my secret identity since you're going to be a part of the family."

Charlie looked down at the little superhero. She still leaned against his thigh. Her weight was insignificant, but her words hit him hard. He'd assumed he was bringing these kids into his family.

The truth was, he had to find a place in their tight-knit community.

Denny might not be his biggest fan. In fact, the kid definitely looked at Charlie as though he was the villain. But now Charlie had at least one ally on his side.

"You know the name Ultra Girl is already taken?" he said. "She's one of Captain Marvel's sidekicks."

"Ugh." Daria placed a knee on Charlie's thigh and hefted herself into his lap. "Who knew the hardest thing about becoming a superhero was choosing a name."

Charlie suppressed a chuckle. He looked again at her cape. It was a mix of white, orange, brown, and gold. Though Charlie suspected the brown wasn't permanent and would come out in the next wash.

"How about Jupiter Girl?" he said, thinking about the gas giant that had always looked like swirling sand in a glass jar to him.

Daria wrapped her spindly arms around his neck. The contact surprised Charlie. It wasn't like when her brother had given him a fake hug. This was real.

"Hmmm, maybe," was her reply.

The little superhero rested her cheek against his

chest for a second. When she pulled away, Charlie was sure she took a piece of his heart with her.

"Really, Charlie? I sneak in here to find you with another woman?"

Savy stood in the doorway to his bedroom. This superwoman presented a very different picture with her hand cocked on her hip than the little super-hero. The grin on Savy's face melted his heart. The gaze she fixed on him was enough to bring him to his knees.

"Relax, Ms. Savy. It's just me, Daria." Daria held up the mask cloth.

"Daria?" Savy pulled on a mask of fake surprise. "You let him in on your secret identity?"

"Yeah," Daria nodded with a grin. "I trust him. He's a hero too, you know."

"I know." Savy nodded, her gaze sparkling with love as she looked at him. "He's been my hero for a long time."

16

"You missed a couple of strands."

Foxy wasn't even looking at Savy as she said it. So she also missed the glare as Savy tucked the loose pieces of hair that hadn't made it into her hastily redone ponytail.

"I don't need to be psychic to know what you were up to."

"Shut up." Savy bumped her sister's shoulder. All that got out of the annoying little fortune teller was a snort and a smirk.

Some mystic she was. Of course, if you put two long-lost loves within the same vicinity, kissing was definitely going to occur. Which would easily lead to a few strands of hair going astray.

Duh!

"What you need to be focusing your energies on is your certification," Savy said.

"No worries," Foxy shrugged. "I have a real good feeling about that."

"Fox, we need more than a feeling if we want to get the certification for elevated care."

Traditional foster care was hard on both kids and families. When a child who had faced trauma was tossed into that mix, it was a recipe that rarely worked out in the kid's favor. That's where elevated care workers came in.

Foxy had the temperament for it. Over the year she'd been working in the system, Foxy had gotten through to kids who'd had very troubled paths. Unfortunately, those kids couldn't come and stay at Bright Horizon's because Foxy's knack for getting through to troubled youth remained on a volunteer basis and not an official one.

"Relax," coo'd Savy's baby sister. "It's all going to work out by the end of the month. Trust me."

Savy wasn't one for predictions. Mainly because Foxy got as many of her foretelling right as she did wrong. The main fortune Foxy had misjudged? That the three James sisters would finally be together now that they were no longer a singing trio. That trio had turned into one solo act.

Savy had never been sure if it was meant to be a duo.

"Fox, are you sure this is what you want?"

Foxy turned to her sister with a quizzical look. Her screwed features were funny to Savy. Hadn't Foxy seen this question coming?

"I can sing whenever and wherever I want, Sav. These kids need me here."

Okay, so this was one of those times her sister's psychic abilities were eerily correct.

"Tricksy will be home soon," Foxy continued. "We're all going to be one big happy family. Soon. Not yet, but soon."

"Ms. Savy!"

Savy turned her attention to Miguel. The kid had a forklift in his hands and hay in his hair.

"I feel like this is slave labor," Miguel grumped.

Denny shoveled a forkful of hay that only narrowly missed Miguel. "No, it's more like indentured labor because we only have to do it for a certain amount of years before we gain our freedom at age eighteen."

"That's a very good distinction, Denny," said Savy. "And what era did indentured servitude happen in history?"

The chores were character building, but she also

had to get the school lessons in where she could during these summer months. Denny narrowed his eyes at her as he scooped up another pitchfork of hay. The kid was smart enough to aim the hay into a pile instead of at her feet.

"Indentured servitude didn't end until the early twentieth century," said Miguel. "But don't indentures need to sign a contract? We didn't sign a contract."

"You can't legally sign a contract until you're eighteen." That came from Charlie.

Even though she'd just left him, the sight of him swaggering up to her made Savy's breath catch. The man was just too beautiful for words. And he was all hers.

"These are your chores," said Charlie. "You do them because this family is a team."

"This isn't a family," said Denny.

Charlie didn't bother responding to the kid. Neither did Savy. She knew it would take some time for Denny to warm up. He was still warming up to her. Not all foster kids came around to trusting their foster parents. But that was okay. Savy would keep the kid safe and prepare him for the world so long as he was in her care. And now Denny had the perfect male role model to look up to.

"Mr. Charlie, can we visit with Duff now that you're here?" said Daria.

The girl stood at the entrance to the pen. LaTisha stood by her side, already fumbling with the latch.

"You finished your chores?"

"Yes, sir," said both girls, bobbing their heads.

"You girls can sit on the fence while he eats," said Charlie. "I'll show you how to brush his mane in a minute."

Daria and LaTisha scrambled up onto the fence nearest the horse. They made clucking noises at the horse while he ate. Duff swished his tail in response, a clear sign of annoyance. Savy didn't blame the animal. He likely wanted to eat his breakfast in peace.

The sound of tires broke the peace of the morning into even more little pieces. A dark sedan ambled to a stop at the front of the house. A man in an ill-fitting suit climbed out of the driver's side with a manilla envelope in his hands and started toward them. When he got closer, Savy recognized him.

"What's he doing here?" said Daria from her place on the fence. "He's a villain. He can't be in our secret lair."

"He's not a villain," said Savy.

At least she hoped Mr. Davidson wasn't a villain. She and the government official were on the same side. They each wanted what was best for these children. Hopefully, what the man carried in that manilla envelope would prove he was an ally.

"I've brought the provisional license," said Mr. Davidson, holding up the envelope.

Savy pressed her hands to her heart. She hadn't realized it was beating so wildly until she felt the kick of the organ against the palms of her hands.

"We got it?" Savy's words were a question, an exclamation, and a prayer of gratitude all in one.

Charlie pulled her into his side and kissed the top of her head. It was all happening. She was going to keep these kids together. She was going to have a forever home here at the Flying Cross Ranch. And she was going to marry the man beside her. It all made her heart beat impossibly faster.

"Since the Flying Cross Ranch was approved in the past as a care facility," said Mr. Davidson, "it made the way forward easier."

Savy's fingers shook as she took the manilla envelope from Mr. Davidson. The documents inside made it all real. It made it official.

"But wait," Savy looked closer at the last page.

"There's a mistake. The provisional license is only for four kids. We have five."

Mr. Davidson sighed. He raised his head and looked pointedly at something over Savy's shoulder. Not something. Someone.

Savy's heart stopped. It was a painful feeling going from one hundred miles a second to zero. She knew without it being said what was about to happen.

"After reviewing her medical records, we think Daria Myers will do better in a rehabilitation foster home with elevated care."

For a full sixty seconds, the only sound that could be heard was Duff's chewing and the *swish swish* of his tail. Then the soft thud of a pitchfork being thrown against the ground.

"You're not taking my sister away."

Denny marched purposefully toward Mr. Davidson. His normally pinched features filled with outrage. Before Savy could grab him, Charlie had a hold of the boy.

"Wait, Denny," Charlie said. "We're going to figure this out."

"There's nothing to figure out," said Denny, trying to dodge Charlie's hold. "You said this could be our forever home. You're a liar. You're both liars like all the rest of them."

The accusation must have stung Charlie because Denny dodged and broke free of Charlie's hold. Before the kid could get to Mr. Davidson, or whatever he'd intended, a scream came from behind them.

They all turned in time to see Daria leap from the fence, cape flying and mask on, onto the back of Duff. The startled horse reared up on his hind legs with the child on his back. Everything in the whole entire world stopped.

17

---

*S*tanding out in the wide-open space of the ranch with the cool country air flowing all around him, Charlie could not breathe. The sweet scent of honeysuckle was cloying to his tongue. The smell of hay and horses burned his nostrils. He gulped, but there was not enough air to fill his lungs.

Charlie's heart beat an erratic pattern as Daria's little body sailed up a couple of feet into the air. Her cape billowed around her torso as though it would save her from the fall. It wouldn't. It couldn't. It was only fabric, too thin to cushion the blow.

The shouts that came from Denny's throat were deep and panicked. It cracked the boy's veneer, exposing the softness beneath his tough exterior.

Savy's scream pierced Charlie's heart. His first instinct for as long as he could remember had always been to run directly to her, to shield his love from any pain that dared come near her. Not this time.

By the time Daria had raised up on the fencing and prepared to leap, Charlie had been in motion. He'd vaulted over the fence just as she'd landed on Duff's bare back. When the horse reared, tossing her off his back, Charlie had been a step behind.

Daria landed on the solid earth with a thud that was louder than her brother's and Savy's cries. The little girl landed a yard away from him. The only thing Charlie could do was to put himself between her and the horse.

To his left, Duff walked off to the opposite end of the pen. His tail swished as though fighting off an annoying gnat. He ducked his head for another bite of hay. His wide eyes went half closed as he relaxed back into his morning meal.

Charlie stepped to his right, where Daria lay curled into a ball. He had to fight his instincts to scoop the girl up to his chest lest she was severely injured. His chest constricted as he knelt down to her, still unable to take in enough air.

Daria's lips parted. She opened her mouth wide

and sucked in the lungful of air that eluded Charlie. Her eyes popped open, and she stared at Charlie, a tear forming at the corner of each eye.

"Daria, what on earth were you doing?" Savy's voice was shaky as she came up behind them. "You could've killed yourself."

"I was trying to fly away, like Mr. Charlie," said Daria. "So that villain wouldn't kidnap me."

Daria sat up. There was no wincing or constriction in her movements. Just a bruise on her shin where she'd met with a rock. It was a miracle the girl was unharmed.

"I've seen enough," said Mr. Davidson. He'd pulled out a notepad from his suit jacket and was furiously scratching on the yellow paper. "I thought you'd be a positive influence, Captain Matthews, but I can see I was wrong. She's coming with me."

"You're not taking my sister." Denny started toward the government official.

It was the second beast to rear up today. Luckily, this time, Charlie made it to the kid before any damage could be done. He caught Denny around the waist and hauled him against his chest. The kid struggled like Charlie was the enemy. His arms and legs flailing to get at his target.

"Don't make it worse," Charlie whispered in Denny's ear. "I got this."

Denny took a deep breath. His small chest expanded. When he exhaled, there was a modicum of calm, but his features were still screwed up in mutiny.

Charlie chanced letting him go. When he did, the kid held still. Though Charlie was certain he was on borrowed time.

Savy held Daria in her arms, checking every inch of her flesh and joints. The other kids were on the other side of the fence with Foxy, holding as still as insects under inspection, fear and uncertainty shining brightly in their eyes.

Charlie turned his attention to the government official. "Mr. Davidson, the kids are still learning the rules of the ranch. You can't let one mistake inform your entire judgment."

"It's not just one mistake," the man said. "My job is to do what's in the best interest of these kids. Daria is going to need more specialized care that I don't believe you can give her."

"If you take her, you're taking me too," said Denny.

Charlie stepped in front of Denny before he could make it worse. He spread his hands in the universal language of Stop, hoping it would allow calm to enter the scene. Or at least give him a few moments to stall and come up with a plan.

"Let's just all take a breath here," said Charlie. "There's nowhere for you to place her tonight. Since you're closing the only foster home in the city. The nearest one is at least a hundred miles away. Let her stay the night, and we'll talk again in the morning."

Mr. Davidson looked from Charlie, who had his hands spread to Denny, who looked ready to murder him, to Daria, who was sniffling as she clung to Savy.

There was a brief moment where Charlie saw a light of compassion in the man's eyes. But then Mr. Davidson looked down at his notepad. A glance at the words written there dissolved his empathy.

"One more night," he said. "Say your goodbyes. I'll be back in the morning with help."

With that edict, Mr. Davidson stuffed his notepad back inside his ill-fitting jacket. He turned on his heel and marched to his car.

"You're a liar."

Charlie turned to face off against Denny. The boy looked at him with betrayal.

"You said this was a forever home, but you're going to let them take my sister."

"Denny, we're going to figure this out."

The kid wasn't listening. Denny stormed off in the direction of the woods. Charlie decided to let him go blow off some steam. There was an even bigger storm brewing in the dark gray of Savy's eyes.

18

It was silent. Silence in a foster home did not bode well.

Savy kept her eye on the bunkhouse, watching for any movement. So far, all she saw was stillness. All she heard was silence. She wasn't the psychic sister in the James clan. Still, she knew something bad was about to happen.

The reality was that something bad had already happened. The tracks of Mr. Davidson's tires were still visible from the porch, even though the sun had set. Savy had the urge to go and kick rocks until the dirt covered the pattern.

It wouldn't matter. Mr. Davidson was still coming back in the morning to take Daria away. And there was nothing Savy could do about it.

"We're not letting this happen."

The sound of Charlie's voice in her ear was once the most comforting thing to Savy. Over a phone crackling with static. In a letter as she imagined him speaking the words. Directly into her ear as he whispered his undying love to her when they were together.

They were together now. Charlie stood behind her as though he would catch her if she fell. She was the one standing sturdy while the world crashed around her.

"They can't just do that, can they?" Charlie asked.

"She's not ours." The words felt like acid on her tongue. "These kids are wards of the state. I just take care of them."

"You do more than that." Charlie turned her to face him. "You teach them. You care for them. You have their best interests at heart. No one could possibly do this better than you."

He was right. Except Savy didn't just care for these kids. She loved each and every one of them with every fiber of her being.

She hadn't thought she could love another soul apart from her sisters and the man now holding her close in this way. She'd been wrong. Her heart seemed to have no boundaries.

It was only the government who did. The government could come take one of her charges away. Because they were only hers in her heart, not legally.

"We're not letting them take Daria. I promised Denny this was their forever home."

Savy reared back from Charlie. Reflexively, he didn't let her go. He held tight.

"You did what?" she demanded.

"In my heart-to-heart with Denny. I told him this was his forever home. That no matter where he was in his life or the world, he could always come back here."

"You had no right to do that, Charlie. You can't promise these kids forever. They're not ours."

Even as she said those last words, the acid in her stomach burned through her chest.

"We promised each other forever," said Charlie.

"We were kids. Now we're adults. Adults can't make that promise. Not in the foster system."

Charlie opened his mouth. Then closed it. His eyes never left Savy's. They screamed that he did not agree with her assessment. But the words to back him up never came.

The quiet that had permeated the night settled

between them. It grew louder and louder until it itched at her skin.

"I'm going to go and check on them," Savy said.

Charlie reached for her as she took a step past him. Then appeared to think better of it. He brought his hands back to himself and shoved them into his pockets.

The love of her life was standing right by her. There were just inches between them. But it was as though he was miles away.

Savy hated it. But she knew that even though she was arguing with Charlie, and she was angry with him, she knew he would be there in the morning. She could not say the same about Daria. And so Savy trudged into the bunkhouse on her own.

The quiet that greeted her scratched at the acid that had started in her gut, climbed into her chest, and was now making its way up her throat. She wanted to speak, to call out to the kids. The quiet told her to listen carefully.

The quiet broke with the squeaking of a sneaker against the polished hardwood floors.

"Ms. Savy!" Ashton appeared in the doorway, blocking her entry. "I wanted you to listen to this dope rhyme I came up with."

That didn't rhyme. It was another warning.

As Savy sidestepped him, Miguel stepped in. "Ms. Savy, Father Matthews gave me this old cookbook. But I'm not sure what some of these ingredients are. Can you help me?"

Miguel knew Savy couldn't cook. It was the reason he'd picked up his first cookbook. The warning bells were getting louder.

Savy stepped around the young chef, only to be confronted with LaTisha. The girl tugged at the rounded tip of her nose. She'd never been one for lies. Not after Savy had read *Pinocchio* to her.

"They're gone," said LaTisha.

Savy already knew. It was the quiet. That old adage was true when it came to kids.

Silence is golden... unless you have kids, then the silence is just suspicious.

The three kids were silent. Savy didn't even need to look in Denny or Daria's rooms to know that they had run away.

19

"There has to be something else I can do." Charlie gripped the steering wheel as he spoke into the phone.

Montana was not a hands-free state, and Charlie didn't have time to feel guilt over multitasking. There were lives at stake. And so he clutched his ancient cellphone to his cheek as he peered out the passenger window at the sidewalks and into the dark alleys.

He had to find them.

"Sorry, bro, but I don't see what else is to be done?" said his brother Joe from the other end of the line. "From the records I can see, it looks like the kid is in serious trouble."

Charlie heard the *tap tapping* of keys through his

earpiece. He could imagine his brother hunched over a large conference table as he bent the red tape of government software to his will. Unlike Charlie, Joe had seen less field combat and more battles in military war rooms.

Tap, tap, tap. "Multiple instances of running away." *Tap, tap.* "And, wow, have you looked at her medical records?"

"Joe, focus. Can't you find some case precedence where Savy gets to keep her?"

"You know the system doesn't work like that. Savy's not the biological parent or even a relative. It would be easier if she was. It's hard to take kids from their parents. Though I see here, the mother's parental rights have been terminated. There's no mention of the father."

That's why it had been easy for the Matthews to foster and then adopt him and his brothers. They were all lost boys. Lost to deceased parents, terminated rights, or a blank on the birth certificate.

"Look, bro, I gotta go, but I'll keep looking. I suppose I'll be staying in the guest house since my room in the bunkhouse has been commandeered."

Foxy had been right about Joe's coming home in a few days. Apparently, he was leaving his position in the JAG Corp for one closer to home. Though he was quiet about exactly what that was.

"Savy and Foxy are staying in there right now," said Charlie.

There was a clatter on the line like the phone had been dropped onto Joe's keyboard. "Foxy? Foxy James is staying in the guest house?"

"Yeah, she'll be living there when we move them all in starting next week."

"And Foxy is staying in the guest house?"

"Yeah, you got a problem with that? You two have known each other since you were kids."

Joe made a humming noise on the phone. His fingers tapped on the keys but in a pattern that didn't sound like he was typing recognizable words. "Exactly where am I supposed to sleep?"

"There's plenty of room in the big house."

"Along with my father and my newlywed brother? No, thank you."

"Then stay in the guest house with Foxy."

There went that humming and tapping noise again. "It won't be a good look for me. The council is considering appointing me to the vacant District Attorney post after my separation from the military. It won't look good for me to stay with an unmarried woman."

"Look, I don't care where you sleep. Just find legal ground for us to get Daria back."

"You gotta find the kid first."

"I'm looking."

Charlie took a sharp left turn. Just like the last street, he was met with nothing but darkness, not a single soul. It was nearing midnight. They couldn't have gotten far and certainly, would be getting tired. They'd also skipped dinner and would likely be hungry.

"You check the pizza parlor?" asked Joe. "Best place to go for scraps."

It was a good idea. Charlie ended the call. He used both hands to navigate back to Main Street and to one of two pizza parlors in the town. Parking the car in front of the closed shop, Charlie got out and went around back.

It was quiet. Too quiet. No bugs or rodents made a peep. Because there were bigger predators out.

"Daria, keep quiet."

"But I like Mr. Charlie. I want to stay with him. Plus, he'll know it's me since I already told him my secret identity."

Daria appeared from behind a large green dumpster. Her cape hung limply around her small shoulders. Her mask was askew. There was red pizza sauce on her chin.

"Hey, Ultra Girl," said Charlie.

"I decided on Jupiter Girl, like you said."

Daria took a few tentative steps toward him. Then she broke out in a run. Charlie held still, too afraid that the wrong move would send the child running again. When she was within his arm span, he scooped her up and crushed her to his chest.

"You okay? You hurt?"

"No, I'm indestructible."

Her spirit might be indestructible, but not her frail body. There were goosebumps on her arms, and she shivered a bit in his hold.

"You gonna turn us in?" said Denny. He still held back, standing closer to the trash bin. "We'll just run again."

"I believe you," said Charlie. He did not let Daria out of his embrace. Instead, he shifted her to his hip as though she were just a baby. "But look how easy it was for me to find you."

"That's why I keep telling him he needs a secret identity," said Daria, leaning into Charlie with all the trust in the world. Which is why it broke Charlie's heart to say the next thing.

Charlie's gaze locked with Denny's. By the scowl

the kid gave him, Charlie knew that Denny knew the words he was about to say. When Charlie turned to Daria, the little girl was completely guileless.

"They're going to take you away tomorrow," said Charlie.

Daria's little lip quivered. The slight weight of her multiplied in his arms. But he did not let her go. He had to be strong for his family.

Denny stormed up to them. "I'm not letting them take my sister. She's the only family I got."

"What if she wasn't?" said Charlie.

He wanted to reach out to the boy, to include him in the embrace, but Charlie knew there were too many layers of hurt and distrust coating the kid's exterior. That was okay. Charlie was determined to break through. And once he did, Denny would see that Charlie would never hurt him or give him a reason to doubt. They just had to let Daria go for a moment before she could come back and be with them forever.

"I have an idea. But I need you to trust me."

"I trust you, Mr. Charlie," said Daria.

They both looked to Denny. Denny's eyes were hard as they glared at Charlie, but they softened when he looked at his sister.

20

---

*S*avy came into wakefulness with a jolt. There was a warm blanket around her body. Her aching body was curled awkwardly on the living room couch.

She must have fallen asleep here sometime in the night while she waited for word from Charlie. Her phone lay on the coffee table. There wasn't a single alert of a missed call or new text.

Where was he? Where were the children? Her gut tightened into knots to think that Denny and Daria were still out there on the streets alone.

"Relax, my dear. Everything is as it should be."

Father Matthews sat across the room in an old rocking chair. His booted feet were entirely on the ground as he gave himself a little heave to rock forward and back. In his hand was an old bible. His smile was the same pleasant peacefulness Savy had come to know since she was a girl.

Savy had always wondered how he kept that smile in the face of the six little hellions he'd taken into his home. Sure, she'd seen him not smiling many times with a thin line across his features. A handful of times, she'd even seen him cross, his mustached mouth turned upside down. Those looks never lasted long. It was as if the frown was too heavy for him to hold on to.

"The kids are back," said that smiling, peaceful face. "Charlie found them and put them to bed. He told me not to wake you. Said you needed the rest."

Savy sat up and uncurled her legs. They creaked and groaned in protest. She had needed the rest. What she needed more was to pull Daria close to her heart and see with her own eyes that Denny was alright.

But something weighed her down. A question she'd always wanted the answer to but was afraid to ask. "Why didn't you take us?"

Father Matthews's legs were straight, heaving the rocking chair all the way back. He bent his knees, and the chair came to rest forward. The peaceful smile straightened as he regarded Savy.

"Me and my sisters? Why didn't you offer to adopt us, too?"

Father Matthews's mouth turned down into a frown. There was no anger there, just a heavy weight. It lifted before he spoke.

"You know, my wife and I couldn't have kids of our own. You girls had parents. We would never imagine taking kids from their parents."

"They were bad parents; awful parents."

"They tried."

"They failed."

"No, they didn't." His smile was sad, but there was a certainty to the weight of it. "As I told you before, you turned out just as you were meant to be. A siren who calls wounded souls to them. You are a strong, compassionate woman whose life work is to care for the kids that society doesn't know what to do with. You won't fail these kids because you know what it means to be failed."

He was right, but... "I still think I could've learned that lesson while on this ranch."

Father Matthews chuckled, his legs straightening as he began to rock once more. "My boys were broken when they came to me. They were each like wild horses untrusting of humankind. Much like your young Denny."

Savy looked out the window. Standing in front of the porch, she saw Charlie and Denny talking. Denny didn't look as though he hated Charlie completely. What had he done to the boy?

"Besides," Father Matthews continued, "I always knew you were destined to be my daughter. One of the first things my son said to me was that he'd vowed to love you until his dying day."

Savy's legs didn't creak as she straightened. She walked over to Father Matthews on sure legs. He ceased his rocking so that she could reach down and give him a strong hug.

When she pulled away, he was grinning at her as though the two were in on a secret. Savy was certain there was nothing this man didn't already know. Had he known she would one day be in this spot? Watching over her as she slept? Holding her tight as she let go her worries? Bringing to him the next generation of troubled youth whom he would have a hand in healing and raising? His sons always said he had a direct line to The Man Upstairs.

Turning back to the front door, Savy made her way outside to the love of her life and the child she wanted to care for. Charlie's head was still bent with Denny's.

Denny looked up at her. Then the kid looked back at Charlie. With a huff, the teen said, "Fine."

He turned and sauntered off. Hands in his pockets. Shoulders hunched as if Charlie had asked him to do chores on a Sunday.

"What was that?" said Savy.

"We've come to an understanding." Charlie caught her in an embrace and pulled her close. "How are you feeling? Rested?"

She didn't have a chance to answer. She didn't even have a chance to ask about Daria. The sound of gravel being kicked up by tires turned her attention to the road where Mr. Davidson's sleek sedan was winding its way toward them.

Savy broke from Charlie's embrace, and for once, he let her go. Savy took a step toward the parking car, but her attention was dragged to the bunkhouse. Daria and Denny were walking hand in hand from the bunkhouse, followed by the other kids. Daria had a backpack strapped to her shoulders as though she was preparing to go to school or camp since it was summer.

Mr. Davidson stepped out of the car with what she could only describe as a goon. A goon who was going to take Daria away. Savy couldn't let that happen. Daria had only just started giving her unsolicited hugs. It would take weeks, maybe even months, for the child to be comfortable enough to give that affection to another person.

But no one was fighting it. LaTisha, Ashton, and Miguel all stopped a few feet away. Denny let go of his sister's hand and let her continue on. Even Charlie had backed up to make a clear way for Daria to go with the goon.

What was going on?

"I'm sorry I was bad, Ms. Savy," Daria said as she wrapped her arms around Savy's middle. "I'll be good while I'm away."

Away? Who said she was going away? Weren't they going to fight?

Daria gave a tug as though she were ready to pull away from Savy. Mr. Davidson and the goon looked on expectantly. Instead of letting her go, Savy locked her arms around Daria and scooped her into her arms. She turned, giving the government men her back, preparing to run. But she was stopped by the most unexpected person.

"Sav," said Charlie. "We have to let her go, but it's not forever."

Forever. There was that word again. Hadn't Charlie promised her forever.

"We're going to get her back. I promise."

Savy wanted to rail that he couldn't promise that to these kids. They weren't hers, not legally. They were in every other way that mattered.

"Trust me, Sav."

Savy's mind and heart were whirling. It was a tornado of emotion. But one thing rang true. She trusted this man with her life. These kids were her life, and so she would trust Charlie with their fate as well.

And so Savy took Charlie's hand, and they faced Mr. Davidson and his goon together.

Charlie hated the pain in Savy's eyes. What he was about to do was going to hurt her. It was unavoidable, but it wouldn't be forever.

"We have to let her go," he said.

Savy didn't say the word. She didn't have to. Her whole body radiated the word no. But she didn't pull away from Charlie. She leaned into him as though it was only his strength that held her up.

He would be strong for both of them. He would be strong for all of them. Because the thought of Daria leaving them hurt him, too.

Charlie wiped the tear from Savy's eye before turning and going down on one knee. He came level to Daria. The little superhero wasn't wearing her mask. She stood as her true self, and she had a tear in her eye as well.

Charlie collected it in his thumb along with Savy's. "You remember the plan?"

Daria opened her mouth to respond. Her lip wobbled. Instead of speaking, she nodded solemnly.

Charlie reached into his pocket and retrieved the medal of honor he'd received. He unclasped the chain and brought it around Daria's tiny neck. The medal hung well below her heart, closer to her gut, where bravery was said to live.

"Now, you remember what I told you?"

"It's not always about the bad guys," said Daria. "Sometimes, you have to focus on saving the good guys."

"That's my girl." He squeezed her shoulder, trying to infuse all the bravery he had into her little body. "We're going to save you."

Daria clutched the Flying Cross medal in her palm. One of the blades peaked out between her thumb and index finger. "I know you will."

"It's time for her to go," said Mr. Davidson.

Charlie straightened to face off with the man. He wanted nothing more than to rail against the unfairness of it all. But as Joe had told him, that wasn't the way. Instead, he was going to do it the government's way. With that in mind, Charlie handed the government official a packet of papers.

"What's this?"

"Petition for adoption," said Charlie.

"You can't adopt her."

"Not Daria. Her brother. We've already started the process to make Dennis Myers a Matthews."

Denny took a deep inhale and let it out slowly. He glanced at his sister and her stiff upper lip. He glanced at Savy and her teary eyes. Then he turned that stone-faced glare on Mr. Davidson and nodded as though conferring his agreement with Charlie.

It was the best Charlie could hope for. Right now. In a matter of weeks, he was certain he and the rebel youth would be off on a fishing trip, or playing catch, or having a heart to heart around a pit fire.

Okay, maybe a couple of months.

"After we adopt Denny, we'll legally be his family. No judge will deny us trying to keep the siblings together when we want Daria to be ours."

Mr. Davidson pursed his lips. A small sigh broke through. It was clear the man wanted what was best for these kids. But he had to follow protocol.

That was fine. They would all bide their time until the paperwork and the protocol tipped in their favor.

With one final longing look, Daria turned to hop in the backseat of the sedan. Her cape billowed behind her as she took a seat. Then the door was closed, the car started, and they were pulling off.

"Adoption?"

Charlie turned to face Savy. Her eyes were still watery, but those tears didn't look sad. They looked surprised.

"It was all that I could come up with on short notice," he said. "I figured you'd be okay with it? But now I'm thinking it might be too much. First marriage, then moving, and now having two kids all at the same—"

Charlie didn't get to finish his statement. Savy leaped into his arms. He caught her at the first instance, not the last moment. She wrapped her arms around him and kissed him. Hard.

"Ew gross," said Miguel.

"I don't think that's appropriate for kids to see," said LaTisha.

"Yeah, they're using tongue, see," said Ash. "Definitely not PG."

No, the short-term plans Charlie had for his long-time fiancée were definitely not PG. Luckily, there was plenty of work they could send these kids off to do that didn't require parental guidance. Pretty soon, he and Savy would need to start the adoption paperwork for each one of them. But first thing was first.

"Hey," said Charlie when he broke the kiss.

"Hey," said Savy, chasing his lips and not letting him get too far.

"You're here."

"I am."

"How long?"

"Forever."

EPILOGUE

"This is your time, Joe. You're definitely the man for the job, and the Board of Commissioners will see it that way."

Captain Joe Matthews swiveled around in his chair. It was a base chair, so it creaked and wobbled. The government spent top dollar on weapons for the men and women who protected their interests. Not so much on ergonomic office furniture.

"This is the first step in what you always wanted." Richard, Joe's soon-to-be campaign manager's voice crackled as it came over the satellite phone line.

Joe had wrapped up his time as a JAG officer in the Armed Forces. He'd spent the last three years serving as legal advisor to one of the military's top commanders. He'd done good work. But this wasn't the work he wanted to do for the rest of his life.

He wanted to continue to serve the people of this great nation. Especially little people like he and his brothers had been. When Charlie had called him a few days ago asking for help with a foster kid, some old spark in Joe's belly had ignited.

This was the reason he'd gone into the law. He'd spent the first years of his life not having a say in his own life. Now that he was grown and had a command of the law, he would never be put in that position again. He could help others in need to find their own voices.

The perfect platform to do that would be as the District Attorney for his county. And maybe, someday, the State Attorney. And then, later in life, something more...

"So, that's the plan," said Richard. "You head home, and we start the schmoozing campaign with the Board of Commissioners."

"I'm headed back home," Joe confirmed. "But when I get there, I first need to help my family with a legal matter."

"What legal matter?"

"Just some help with a foster kid they want to adopt."

"That's..." There was a bit of static over the phone, and a few of Richard's words were lost to the ether. "... great on your resume. It'll definitely convince Commissioner Benson that you're the man for the job."

"I thought you said they all see me as a fit to fill the District Attorney position."

"Yeah, well," Richard hedged as the phone line crackled. "A few need convincing. A good deed like that will convince them. That and you finding the right hometown girl to propose to."

"Propose?" There must've been a disconnect or interference with the line. Joe couldn't have possibly heard that correctly.

"Can't have a bachelor in line for U.S. State Attorney for Montana."

Joe heard that loud and clear. That was his ultimate goal. But marriage?

"I'll work on finding you the right girl," Richard was saying, his voice coming across loud and clear on the phone line. "We just can't have any scandals in the meantime."

"Right. No scandals."

"I'll also have a realtor looking into a condo for you."

"A condo?" asked Joe. "Why would I stay in a

condo when my family has a two thousand acre ranch?"

"Didn't you say there were people staying there?"

"Yeah," Joe said, then added. "Just some foster kids." He hesitated another moment and then conceded. "And my brother's fiancée... and..."

The line crackled again. Joe waited for the interference to die down. It didn't. The connection snapped before Joe could finish his sentence.

What Joe didn't mention was that there was another adult guest staying there as well. But what happened between him and Foxy James was years ago. No reason they couldn't be on the same ranch. In the same guest house.

None at all.

You've met Foxy.
So you know her and her psychic abilities are a
scandal waiting to happen for Joe.
Wonder if Foxy will predict what will happen when
Joe returns?
Find out in *His Vow to Treasure*,
Book Two in the Flying Cross Ranch Romances!

ALSO BY SHANAE JOHNSON

Shanae Johnson was raised by Saturday Morning cartoons and After School Specials. She still doesn't understand why there isn't a life lesson that ties the issues of the day together just before bedtime. While she's still waiting for the meaning of it all, she writes stories to try and figure it all out. Her books are wholesome and sweet, but her are heroes are hot and heroines are full of sass!

And by the way, the E elongates the A. So it's pronounced Shan-aaaaaaaa. Perfect for a hero to call out across the moors, or up to a balcony, or to blare outside her window on a boombox. If you hear him calling her name, please send him her way!

You can sign up for Shanae's Reader Group and receive a FREE NOVELLA in this world at

http://bit.ly/ShanaeJohnsonReaders

Also By Shanae Johnson

a Flying Cross Ranch Romance

His Vow to Love

His Vow to Treasure

His Vow to Adore

His Vow to Trust

His Vow to Respect

His Vow to Defend

The Silver Star Ranch Romances

His Pledge to Honor

His Pledge to Cherish

His Pledge to Protect

His Pledge to Obey

His Pledge to Have

His Pledge to Hold

The Rangers of Purple Heart

The Rancher takes his Convenient Bride

The Rancher takes his Best Friend's Sister

The Rancher takes his Runaway Bride

The Rancher takes his Star Crossed Love

The Rancher takes his Love at First Sight

The Rancher takes his Last Chance at Love

The Brides of Purple Heart

On His Bended Knee

Hand Over His Heart

Offering His Arm

His Permanent Scar

Having His Back

In Over His Head

Always On His Mind

Every Step He Takes

In His Good Hands

Light Up His Life

Strength to Stand

The Rebel Royals series

The King and the Kindergarten Teacher

The Prince and the Pie Maker

The Duke and the DJ

The Marquis and the Magician's Assistant

The Princess and the Principal